Smooth Talking Texan

Smooth Talking Texan

A Rossis of Whiskey River Romance

Katherine Garbera

TULE
PUBLISHING

Dedication

To my dad, Dave Smith, who always has my back even if I'm the one in the wrong, always ready to stand by my side and always making me laugh. I stole one of his sayings for Colby's dad in this book. But it's one of many funny things my dad says that always just lightens the mood and keeps us all laughing. So in the words of Dave Smith…you know how it goes, first your money, then your clothes!

Love you, Dad.

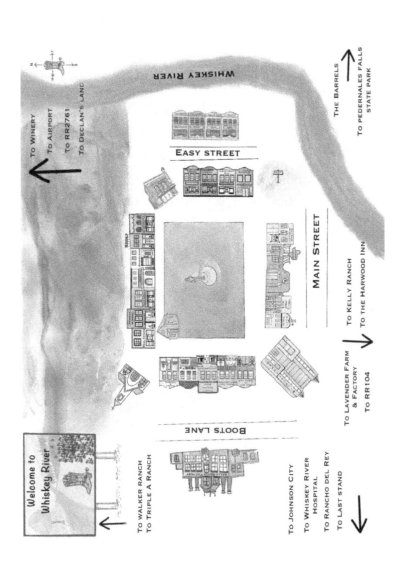

Chapter One

COLBY TUCKER HAD been in love with Ollie Rossi since the first day he'd pulled his battered pickup into the space next to hers and leaned out the window to introduce himself.

He had a square jaw that was more often than not covered in stubble, thick brownish hair that curled when he let it go too long without a haircut, which to be honest, he almost always did. He wore faded, worn blue jeans that hugged the curve of his butt and his long legs. His boots were quality but well used, and he always wore a straw cowboy hat on his head. He usually wore faded jeans and a T-shirt with one of his favorite bands—Coldplay or ZZ Top—and maybe it was her overactive libido, but those tees seemed to hug his muscled biceps and pecs like a second skin. He looked like her version of a cowboy wet dream whenever he walked toward her, and it was all she could do to pretend to be blasé.

He'd friend-zoned her after that first meeting and seeing how quickly the buckle bunnies rotated through his trailer weekend after weekend when they were on the road with the rodeo, she knew she should be happy about it. But she'd be lying if she said she was. She'd had more than her fair share of hot dreams about Ollie.

His real name was Olivier. Sort of hoity for a rodeo cowboy and she'd never seen him as anything other than Ollie. Shep barked and she glanced at her husky. He nudged his empty water bowl toward her. She nodded. That's right she'd been filling up his food and water bowls when she'd gotten distracted by Ollie pulling in next to her in the large field that the rodeo participants used as a campground.

She filled Shep's bowls, petting him before she put them down and then turned away from the window. She'd decided that this was the year she got over Ollie Rossi. To be fair, it had been one hell of a lot easier not to think about him when she'd been home in Georgetown over the winter months when the rodeo wasn't in session but here it was March 1st and she realized she hadn't made one damned inch of progress on getting over that man.

She heard the rap on her door, knew it was him. He always liked to have a catch-up after they'd been apart for a while. Truth was she loved it too. But honestly, she wished she could just see him as a friend the way he saw her. It would make her life so much easier. She needed to get over him and move on.

She opened the door with a smile and almost caught her breath at how handsome he was. His bright blue eyes in that olive tanned face with the thick curls on the top of his brown-black hair. His firm mouth lifted in an answering smile.

"Hey, Colby-girl, missed ya," he said, stepping into her trailer and giving her a hug.

Sap that she was, she closed her eyes and breathed in the scent of his aftershave, something outdoorsy and sort of woodsy that she had never smelled on anyone else. His arms dropped and she stepped back still tingling form the body-to-body contact. Shep stopped eating to come over and greet one of his favorite people.

This.

Even her dog was hung up on Ollie. She had to get herself sorted. She'd even let her mom set her up when she'd been home, hoping that maybe she would meet someone new who would distract her. But the truth was every guy she'd met didn't measure up to Ollie. Her never-boyfriend.

"Missed ya too," she said. "Want some coffee?"

"Love some. That drive was long," he said as Shep trotted back to his food station.

Colby went to her pod machine and took out the dark roast pods she kept just for him and made him a cup. He sat down on the couch in the "living" area of her trailer. She brought his coffee over to him while he told her about a book he'd been reading. She chatted with him like they were friends. But in her heart she knew that this was slowly killing her.

Her mom had pointed out a few of the guys that she'd

set Colby up with were her type or had been before this one-sided love affair she had with Ollie. She had to cut him out of her life. It would be hard of course, she thought as she listened to the soothing sound of his deep voice. She was a barrel racer, and he was a rodeo clown for the bull riders. They were going to run into each other a lot. But she had to do this.

"Sounds interesting," she said when he stopped talking, not having heard a single thing he said.

"Really? I wouldn't have thought that you were interested in that time period. But I'll bring the book over later so you can borrow it," he said. "Great coffee. Thanks."

"You're welcome."

A sort of silence fell, and she took a breath. She'd just tell him they needed to have a little space.

"So—"

"Um—"

They both spoke at the same time. She shook her head. "Sorry about that. What were you saying?"

He smiled at her and she saw that cracked front tooth of his, the one that she was always curious about but had never asked about. "Ladies first."

And she chickened out. She wasn't ready to tell him she didn't want to hang out anymore. "Do you want a cookie with your coffee?"

"I'd love one," he said. "But before you get up, I have something to ask you and I want you to know it's okay to say no."

Was it something serious? It had to be. Why else would he say it like that?

"What is it? You know I'd do anything for you," she said, knowing no matter how much she wished it were otherwise that was the truth.

"I need you to be my fake fiancée at my brother's wedding."

OLIVIER ONLY FELT truly alive when he was back on the rodeo circuit. Here he wasn't the youngest Rossi son who hadn't lived up to expectations. Here he was just Ollie. A rodeo clown who was taken at face value. And no one made him feel more at home than Colby.

He wasn't the prep school kid with the wealthy parents, famous, successful brothers...he was just himself. A simple cowboy who had nothing other than his pickup truck and trailer. That's all he needed.

He wasn't going to front, Colby was hot. The kind of woman that a different man would have gone after hard and fast, making her his from the moment they'd met. But she was a complication he didn't want. He genuinely liked her and didn't want to add her to the list of people he'd let down. He wouldn't allow himself that.

He'd tried to be what everyone wanted once and it had backfired. The simple truth was he liked Colby and didn't want to ruin the friendship they had.

He needed her. Or at least what she would represent to his mama, who was bound and determined to see all of her sons married and settled in Whiskey River. He had been beyond pissed at his parents when they'd bought a ranch in the Texas Hill Country and moved there. He had liked Texas being his. But it no longer was.

Jock had opened a restaurant in Last Stand and then Nico had gotten engaged to a local girl from Whiskey River and the place where he could be himself and not have to face his family's understated expectations and disappointment was gone.

And now that his parents were closer, they wanted more of his time and as much as he wished it were otherwise, he'd always tried to be a dutiful son. But every time, he'd fallen short. He knew he had to show up to Nico's wedding. He also knew that unless he brought a date—a serious date—his mom was going to have a string of single women to set him up with when he returned.

His mom was cagey and determined to fix the broken part inside of him—he'd give her that. He knew she was doing it out of love, which was why he'd indulged her at Christmas, but he wasn't going to fall for some small-town girl and fall into line the way his brothers had.

The dates would be couched as a favor for a friend whose daughter needed someone to move a sofa or coffee with a friend's daughter who had just come off a bad breakup…actually that one hadn't been too bad. She had been as uninterested in being set up as he'd been.

But being home for the entire month of December had confirmed that his mom was in serious match-making mode. There was no two ways about it. Both of his elder brothers settling down hadn't soothed her need for grandchildren, it had simply magnified it.

"I'm sorry, what?" Colby asked.

He shook his head, putting his coffee mug on the table. "I know it's preposterous to think in the twenty-first century that I'd be asking you to be my fake fiancée but the truth is my mom is on overload matchmaking mode right now. If I don't do something to divert her, I'm going to be 'accidentally' set up on a first date every night I'm home."

She leaned back and crossed her arms over her chest, looking at him from under those long, thick eyelashes of hers. She wasn't amused, and for the first time since they'd met he had the feeling he'd made her mad.

"Why not just find a real girlfriend? You don't seem to have much trouble with the ladies," she said.

"I don't. But Mom will know I'm not serious about any of them."

"And she'll think you're serious about me?" she asked.

He wasn't sure how to answer that. The fact of the matter was that Colby had this girl-next-door quality to her and an innate kindness that would appeal to his mom. Hell, it appealed to him and if he were interested at all in settling

7

down, he would have asked her out.

But he wasn't.

And given the fact that she didn't seem inclined to go the domestic route, he thought Colby might be the right choice, but her reaction was giving him signs that were all pointing to wrong.

"Yes. You're not a casual sort of woman, Colby. I'm sure I'm not telling you anything new," he said.

"You're right, I'm not," she admitted. "But that's even more reason for us not to play games."

"Why? It's clear to me that there's something standing in the way of you getting serious. It seems to me you're as averse to it as I am."

"I'm not averse," she said, stiffly.

"Then what? I can't imagine you would be single if you didn't want to be," he said. This conversation was getting away from him. He hadn't meant to discuss her dating life at all. He'd sort of figured she'd just say yes and then they'd go for a ride with Shep.

"I like someone I can't have," she said.

"Oh?"

"Yeah."

He looked over at her. Who could she like that wouldn't want her back? What man would be that dumb? "Maybe this will be a good distraction for you."

She turned away from him and then stood up and paced to the small window over the sink and looked out. He had no idea what she was thinking. He seemed to be off his game today, which wasn't like him.

This was all a mistake. Colby was one of the few people on the planet that he could count on. She had always just accepted him as he was. He didn't want to fuck this up.

He got up and walked over to her, putting his hand on her shoulder. She turned, and her long braid brushed the back of his hand. It was soft and sent a tingle up his arm. Her lips were parted and, when her eyes met his, he realized perhaps for the first time just how pretty she was. He had the urge to kiss her and stepped back, realizing he had lost all his damned sense.

"Sorry. I'm an idiot, which I know you already knew. That was a dumb thing to ask. I'll figure it out."

He turned to walk away but she caught his hand in hers. He turned back, his gaze going to her mouth, which now that he'd thought about kissing her, he couldn't tear his eyes from.

"I didn't say no."

HE WAS OFFERING her the worst sort of temptation. Any other man and she'd just say no. But this was Ollie. And maybe this was what she needed to get over him. For the first time since they'd met, he'd ticked her off with his casual assumption that she'd do it because she had no one else. And it had made her realize that she'd always seen him through the lens of this man she wanted and couldn't have.

Perhaps Ollie in real life was a man she wouldn't want. If she did this…she'd either finally be free of him, or… She shook her head. This would work out. Plus, if he was her fake fiancé, he wouldn't be bringing home buckle bunnies all season long…would he? No, he wouldn't. She was going to have to establish some rules to make this situation work for her. And just to be clear, her subconscious reiterated, she was doing this to get over him for good.

"Are you saying yes?"

She shrugged and dropped his hand. "I'm not sure. When is the wedding?"

"June."

"June? That's months away," she said.

"I know. But my family purchased a table for Boots & Bangles, which is next weekend—March 19. So if I'm going to convince my mom that you and I are a couple, it would be good to start now. She's already got a friend's daughter lined up for me. She doesn't want any odd numbers at the table," he said, shoving his hands through his thick hair, which just mussed it and made him look sexy as hell.

She stepped back and shook her head. *Snap out of it, Colby.* "Okay. If I'm going to be your fiancée even for just a short time, you can't bring women back to your trailer while we are on the circuit," she said.

"Fair enough. But you have to go out with me after the rodeo on Saturday nights—that way I won't be tempted to pick someone up," he said.

"Do you really have so little self-control?" she asked.

"Are you really afraid to go to a bar with me after the rodeo?" he countered.

"No."

Yes, totally yes. Tequila and Ollie didn't sound like a good combo to her. Of course, she could just order beer or club soda…she'd cross that bridge when she came to it.

"Anything else?"

"I'm not really good at lying," she admitted.

"I know. That's why I have a ring in my pocket, and I'm prepared to actually propose to you with the understanding that after Nico's wedding you break it off with me and go back to your regular life."

He was going to propose? She knew it was fake, but she still felt a thrill deep inside of her and she knew this had to end. Did she end it right now or take the next few months…March until June…to be with him, hope that she'd discover he wasn't the male fantasy she'd made him into in her head. He was already sort of doing it. Her ideal Ollie would never ask her to fake-marry him.

"Okay." The words came out without her really thinking about it. But she knew she'd regret it forever if she didn't play this game. Who knew, he might fall for her.

Stop.

She couldn't entertain that notion. This was a strict getting-over-Olivier-Rossi plan. Look for his warts, shortcomings and weaknesses. Find the real man behind the sexy ass, easy smile and get the f—over him.

"Really?" he asked, sounding a little surprised.

"Yes. I'll do it," she said.

"Great. You're the best, Colby-girl," he said, hugging her and she put her arms around him. His hug still felt as great as it always did, but it didn't hurt as much as it usually did because she knew that in June, she wouldn't be hugging him like this. She'd be over him and moving on.

"I think you should probably stop calling me Colby-girl," she said. "It makes me sound like your pal instead of your girlfriend."

"Fair enough," he said. "It's going to be hard to stop doing it."

She knew it. She'd miss it. But this was how she was going to extricate him from her heart. One tiny piece at a time.

"Thank you."

"So, do you want to go for a ride? Now that we've gotten my craziness out of the way," he asked.

She looked at her watch and realized they had the rest of the afternoon free. The rodeo practice and events didn't begin until the next day. "I'd like that. Meet you by the corral in fifteen minutes?"

"Sure," he said, starting to walk out of the trailer, but he stopped suddenly. "I really appreciate this."

"I know."

He reached for her, touching the tail of her braid when it

rested on her shoulder. She stood there looking over at him, unsure what he was doing. He leaned in, lowering his head and she realized he was going to kiss her.

She put her hand up and blocked him. "Not that."

"If we are going to expect everyone to believe we are engaged, we'll have to kiss."

"No one is here," she pointed out.

"What if we suck at it?" he asked. "Better to find out in private than in front of an audience."

"Yeah," she said. "I can't do this right now. Can we put it off until after our ride?"

He nodded and stepped back from her. "You're right. So far, I've made our reunion all about me and what I want. I'm sorry. Let's go for our ride and I'll try to be the man you've come to expect."

He walked out of the trailer and she watched him go, realizing that the real side she'd just glimpsed wasn't making her hate him. In fact, his understanding just made her like him more. But she knew she'd find things she didn't like. She was determined to. It was the only way she was going to get over him.

Chapter Two

OLLIE SADDLED UP his mustang, Parker, and waited for Colby. He was still trying to figure out what exactly had happened in her trailer. Somehow his buddy had suddenly turned hot and kissable, and he couldn't stop thinking about her mouth. Not at all what he was planning on.

His father always said best laid plans were easiest wrecked and to be honest since his dad said stuff like that all the time, he tended to ignore it. But this time…well, it seemed the old man might be on to something. He had a ring in his pocket so he could propose to her properly because he knew his mom and sister would ask about that. Also, he wanted everything to seem flawless…which it had right up until he'd noticed her lips.

Parker whinnied and butted his head against Ollie's chest. He petted the horse and tried to tell himself he hadn't made a huge mistake. But he felt like he had done something stupid.

If he wasn't planning to lie to his entire family, he would give his brother Jock a call and talk this out. But that route was now closed, and he couldn't talk to the rodeo guys he hung out with because Colby was part of this community. He was stuck with his own counsel and right now that didn't seem like the best course of action.

He heard a yip and turned to see Shep racing toward them, Colby and her paint Lola right behind them. He bent to pet Shep and then Shep and Parker said howdy the way animals did. Colby had put on her heavy shearling jacket and had on a brown cowboy hat that matched her jacket. She waved at him as she approached.

Instead of talking a mile a minute to him, she was quiet and reserved. Hell, with his proposal, he'd already changed the dynamic between them.

Hey, genius, did you really think it wouldn't?

Well, sort of, he thought. He'd thought that they could have fun as friends and just hang out more than they did at the rodeo, but he was beginning to realize that had been dumb.

"I hope you don't mind but I packed a picnic," he said. "Figured it'd be nice to stop up on the ridge when we get there."

"I don't mind if you brought those delicious Louisiana sandwiches you make," she said.

Muffulettas. "Of course. It's the one thing I can make."

She started laughing. "You do okay with coffee."

"Dang, Colby-girl, you know how to hurt a man," he said.

She shook her head and continued laughing and for the first time since he'd asked for a favor, he felt he was with his friend again.

"Just dropping truth bombs like I do," she said. "You ready to ride?"

"I am," he said, offering his hands to her as a stirrup so he could give her a leg up. She took it and took her saddle like she'd been born to ride, which she had. Colby's dad was a legendary three-time PBR champ and her mom had been a champion barrel rider just like Colby.

She whistled for Shep as Ollie got on Parker and they took off across the meadow. This was the first stop on the rodeo tour. They were part of a weekly or local tour that hit towns throughout Oklahoma, Texas and Arkansas through spring and then in the summer they went to the bigger rodeos in those same states. He liked the circuit. It was a nice way to rodeo without the bigger crowds and egos. Not that the riders on the circuit didn't think they were all that.

"Um…I was thinking since we're going to be engaged do you think you could come home with me for Easter? My mom had three blind dates lined up for me when I was home at Christmas."

"What is it with our moms? Sure, I can do that. I'll probably have to go home at Easter too—maybe we can figure out a way to do both?"

"Maybe. My family lives in Hill Country too," she said. "Georgetown. So conceivably we could drive between the two."

"Sounds like a plan," he said.

"I'm thirty this year so my mom is starting to get worried," Colby said. "She even suggested freezing my eggs so that I'll still be able to give her grandkids. My daddy just shook his head and walked out of the room. But I'm telling you, Ollie, it was like talking to a crazy person."

He had the feeling that a fake engagement was going to make both of their moms happy at first but might cause more pain in the end. "My mom wants all her kids settled. And since Angelica lives in town, she gets the bulk of the marrying vibes but when I'm home...she sort of just goes on a frenzy."

"Yeah that. Mom also thinks I should stop riding. I don't know what I'd do if I wasn't on tour. I know the money's not great but I've got all I need right here," she said.

"Coaching young riders?" he suggested. "I know you mentioned you'd been looking at buying some property."

"I also mentioned it to my daddy, so my Christmas present was forty acres of undeveloped land in Hill Country. That is a possibility. Still not sure I want to stop riding," she said.

She had a plan, which made him realize that all he had was a fake engagement so he could keep traveling around with the rodeo. He'd been rambling for so long, he wasn't sure he knew how to stop. What would he do if he did? He had other interests and earned money from his consultancy.

But the truth was he liked this life. Here he was beholden to no one. Here he didn't have to worry about the restrictions of a life he wasn't sure he wanted.

His father would offer him a job in the family business. The import/export shipping company that had been in their family for generations, but he'd originally run away to the rodeo because he hadn't wanted that.

But he didn't know what he wanted. When he looked at the future all he saw was…nothing. He saw himself running from the same life his brothers had and the one his parents had always wanted for him.

COLBY DECIDED TO ignore Ollie's suggested scheme and just pretend that she was riding with a friend. But that wasn't working. All she could think of was that he had analyzed the many women in his life and come to the conclusion she was the one he could ask to be his fake bride.

She wasn't too sure that was compliment.

She knew he thought of her as a buddy but still he had to guess she was a woman and had feelings. Didn't he?

"Why did you ask me to help you out?" she blurted when they'd stopped for lunch. He was spreading out his picnic blanket, which she'd seen many times before, and pulling food out of his saddle bags.

"What do you mean?"

She took a deep breath. It was one thing for her to have

her secret crush/obsession with him, but this was something different. "Why did you think I'd say yes? Do you think I'm not interested in dating?"

"No. Why would I think that?"

"Not sure."

"You mentioned you want someone who's not available. I guess I sort of always sensed that," he said. "I mean from the beginning you and I have been great friends, but you never put any romance vibes out…"

She hadn't?

"You made it clear you thought of me as your good friend," she said. "I didn't want to make you uncomfortable."

"So you thought about kissing me?"

"What?" This was getting totally out of control. She wasn't sure that spending more time with Ollie was going to be a good idea. In fact the more she thought about it, the dumber it seemed. She'd been in a mood during their ride and so far, that hadn't made her want him any less.

"Sorry. It's just I thought something passed between us in your trailer… I hadn't realized what a kissable mouth you have before."

WHAT!!!

Her lips felt dry and she was resisting the urge to lick them because he was staring at her mouth. Her ordinary sort of regular mouth. Suddenly she wondered what he saw. She wanted to pull out a compact and check except she'd never been the kind of woman to carry one around.

"Yeah, so, seems I made it awkward again."

"No…I mean yes. Totally yes. But I'm glad you said it. I have thought about kissing you," she admitted.

"Good."

"Why?"

He set the food on the blanket and walked over to her, not standing too close, but he was definitely in her personal space. "If we are going to convince my family you're my fiancée, we are going to have to touch, kiss and seem intimate."

He had leaned in when he said that last part, and she felt her heart start to race. He was describing everything she'd ever fantasized about with him. Everything she'd ever wanted—he was offering. But temporarily. Was that enough? Was this going to leave her more broken and scarred than she could handle? Was this something she could say no to?

She couldn't. She wanted it. Even if it was only for a few months. She'd dreamed of being in his arms so many times and now he was admitting to wanting to kiss her and she didn't care if this was the stupidest thing she'd ever done, she wasn't walking away. Not now.

She took a deep breath. She had to do something to protect herself from this situation—opportunity??—before she got in too deep.

"What if…one of us starts to fall for the other?" she

asked.

He reached out and touched her braid where it lay on her shoulder, picking up the end and running it through his fingers. "I guess we'd have to be clear with the other one. I don't want to hurt you and I don't want to get hurt myself. I guess we'd both have to just agree to let each other know if we have to walk away."

She nodded. "But I'd still have to honor my promise to go to your brother's wedding."

"Well, that is what I would like. What do you think? Is this something you could do?"

She took a deep breath and licked her lips at last because they were still tingling. This could either be her chance to make him fall for her or to get over him. Either way she'd be in a better place than she was right now. As if she was ever going to say no to being Ollie's fake fiancée.

She knew she wasn't.

"Yes. I think we can do this," she said.

"Great," he said, lifting his hand from her braid. He cupped her face and ran the pad of his thumb along her lower lip. "Should we seal our bargain with a kiss? Earlier I know you weren't ready…"

Sensual shivers were coursing through her and she knew that this was the moment of truth. Cowgirl up. She had never been the kind of woman to walk away from a challenge and now when the stakes were so high, she definitely wasn't going to.

She opened her mouth and licked the tip of his thumb. His eyes widened and he shifted so he was closer, moving his hand away from her mouth. She felt the brush of his lips against hers.

Damn.

He tasted good. Like this was the best the kiss she'd ever had. She closed her eyes. Maybe it was just that she knew she was kissing Ollie that made it taste so good. But that only intensified everything. His hand was on her waist, drawing her closer, and he must have tipped his head to deepen the kiss, because his tongue brushed over hers and she knew she was lost.

He groaned and lifted his head, and she opened her eyes to look up at him. He shook his head. "Damn, Colby-girl, you are one hell of a kisser."

"You're not so bad yourself."

TAKING A STEP back from Colby was really all he could do. She was playing a part so he couldn't take this any further. Not now. He had a plan and so far nothing was going exactly the way he'd imagined it. He hadn't expected this attraction.

But he refused to let that throw him. He took her hand in his and took a step back, going down on one knee. This was the right moment.

"What are you doing?"

"Proposing...what did you think I was doing?"

"Why?"

"My mom and sister are going to ask you about this. I don't want you to have to lie," he said.

"Okay," she said. Her eyes were wide and she stared at him with a cocktail of emotions in her expression that he couldn't read—and maybe that was a good thing.

"Colby Tucker, you have been one of the best friends I've ever had, and it would be the greatest honor of my life if you said you'd marry me," he said, pulling the ring from his pocket. His hands felt sweaty. He couldn't image how he'd feel if this was real. Of course it was real, sort of.

"Are you sure about this?" she asked. "Once I put that ring on, we will be engaged until I take it off. That means no other women, that means our rodeo family and friends will know..."

He stood up, rubbing his hand on her arm. "I'm sure. But if you're not..."

He hadn't thought of how it might be on the rodeo when they broke up. "Maybe we should keep it a secret while we're here. I don't want you to have deal with the gossip that comes with me."

She chewed her lower lip between her teeth. "That might be best. I mean unless you're planning to leave the rodeo after we break up."

"No, why would I?"

"Well, if we were a real couple both of us wouldn't be

able to stay and work here. I think a secret engagement would be best," she said.

When she put it that way, he did too. Besides he only needed to fool his mom until after Nico's wedding and then hopefully Jock and Delilah or even Nico and Cressida would be expecting and his mom would be diverted.

"I agree. I do want you to wear this ring though. I bought it special for you," he said. "Will you do it?"

"I will," she said.

He took her hand and for the first time noticed how long her fingers were. And slim. She had elegant-looking hands, which shouldn't surprise him. But somehow it did. He slipped the ring onto her ring finger and she looked down at it. It was a simple band that he'd gotten from Tiffany's in New York the last time he'd gone to visit Nico there. He'd been thinking of this plan for a while.

The band was the Tiffany Victoria diamond vine band ring. He'd dipped into his savings to get it for her. He'd gotten it in rose gold because he thought it would look best on her hand. It had alternating solid diamonds with clusters of diamonds in each of the leaves. He wanted her to have something to keep when this was over. He was trying his level best to make this as painless as possible for her. But when he stood there holding her hand and looking down into her eyes, he realized he hadn't even considered the fact of his own chances of falling for her.

Hell, until today in her trailer he hadn't even thought of

kissing her. He almost groaned out loud as he hardened in his jeans and had to shift his stance to make room for his erection. He wanted her.

This was a wrinkle he hadn't foreseen, but he figured it would work to make this lie more believable. And it was important that everyone believe it, he thought. He had made the decision not to marry a long time ago, had realized that love wasn't for him. He'd tried the engagement and the "love" route, but it hadn't worked out. He'd crashed and burned hard and ended up here at the rodeo. Promised himself he wouldn't do that again.

It hadn't been just his own heart that had been broken. It had been the disappointment of the rest of his family. It had been realizing that what he'd always known was true: he was the odd Rossi. He might look like his brothers, have the same drive to excel, but he didn't have the solid grounding that they did.

But friendship and this kind of arrangement would work perfectly, as long as he could remember that it was just temporary.

"This is beautiful, Ollie. I don't know what to say."

"You don't have to say a word. I wanted something that matched your style and this one according to the sales rep resembles the blazing intensity of the night sky...kind of made me remember our last evening ride during the comet shower. Any—"

He broke off as she threw herself in his arms and she

kissed him. It wasn't tentative or a thank you, it was a full-on woman-kissing-her-man kiss. He wrapped his arms around her and took everything she had to give, cupping her butt to draw her more fully against him, arching his hips and rubbing his erection against the notch between her thighs until he realized what he was doing.

He wasn't going to tumble Colby to the blanket and have sex with her. No matter how much his body wanted it. This wasn't about sex. But damn, it could be.

How had he missed this intensity between them? Had he been blind to her?

He lifted his head and stepped back. "So I guess we should eat."

She rubbed her fingers over her lips and then nodded slowly. The sun glinted off the diamonds in her ring and something primitive went through him. He looked at his ring on her hand.

She's mine now.

He shoved those thoughts away. No woman was his. He'd learned that a long time ago and he certainly wasn't going to make a mess of his friendship with Colby by forgetting it. She was doing him a huge favor and he was going to treat her with the respect she deserved.

No matter how much he wanted to treat her as if she were his woman.

Chapter Three

O LLIE LEFT COLBY at her trailer to go and practice with the bull riders. There were a couple of newer riders on the circuit this year and as a rodeo clown he wanted to get to know them. Let them know how he worked. She stood for a millisecond starring at the ridiculously gorgeous ring he'd given her.

It was too pretty, too expensive, too…perfect. A ring she would have selected for herself.

Her original plan to use this time to find his flaws wasn't going to work. She had to make him fall in love with her. Now that he was kissing her, looking at her differently, she could do this. She'd use all the skills she had—except obviously it hadn't worked so far. She needed to pull in the big guns.

She groaned.

F—.

She was going to regret this, but it seemed a day for doing things that she normally wouldn't. She picked up her phone and texted her older sister. Just a quick hey. If Beckett didn't answer then Colby would drop this harebrained scheme.

Of course, Beckett texted right back.

Bossy: *Hey. You okay? You never text? Are Mom and Dad okay?*

Ugh!

Colby: *Everyone's fine as far as I know. I, uh, kind of, I need some man advice.*

Immediately her video chat started ringing and Colby groaned, but answered. She knew Beckett would be all over this.

"Who is it? Tell me everything," Beckett said. The former Ms. Texas was of course perfectly coiffed and made-up even though it was the middle of the afternoon and her sister was a stay-at-home mom.

"A rodeo guy," she said.

"Really?"

"Yes."

"I thought they were all one-night-stand guys. Oh, my goodness, Cole, this is so exciting. I mean I've never pushed—"

"Yeah, right."

"Well maybe a little bit but only because I love you. I thought something was up when you were home but with the kids and the holiday stuff, we never had a chance to just talk."

Colby was really glad that they hadn't talked. She might have mentioned her unrequited crush on Ollie and then this wouldn't have been possible. She put her head in her hand. What was she doing?

"Don't worry, Cole. I got your back," Beckett said, glancing at her watch. "Let me text Albie and let him know I'm not going to be able to do the school run. I want to give this my full attention. I can't believe you are finally into a guy...but you said man advice—"

"Text Albie. I can wait."

She made herself a coffee while her sister texted her nanny. Beckett always tried to be quick, but her sister liked to chat and couldn't say hello in less than five minutes. Colby had never wanted to be her sister, but she envied Beckett the easy way she had with people. The truth was Colby was more comfortable with animals than people—except Ollie. But she needed him to really see her and fall in love with her.

"Okay. Let's hear it," Beckett said.

She hesitated for a moment wondering if she was going to tell her sister the entire truth, but she'd never lied to Beckett and didn't intend to start now. Beckett always had her back. She needed someone to talk her out of this fake engagement. "This is going to sound crazy."

"Girl, when a man is involved it always does."

She laughed, realizing how much she'd missed girl time with her sister since they'd both become so busy with their adult lives.

"Okay. So, I've sort of been crushing on this guy here at the rodeo for the last few years. He totally friend-zoned me when we met and he's usually the one-night-stand or one-weekend man. Just so you don't think I'm totally pathetic, I did intend to get over him this year…but today he asked me for a favor."

"Oh, dear. You don't sound pathetic. Love isn't smart or smooth. What does he want?"

She took a deep breath. "He wants me to be his fake fiancée so his mom will stop fixing him up. I said yes."

"Of course, you did. What's next?"

"Oh, Beck, he asked me to marry him, like got down on his knee after we'd been riding and asked me—said he wanted me to have a good story to tell his mom and sister—but then he kissed me, and it felt real."

"Of course it did. He probably just doesn't realize he wants you for real," her sister said.

"Beck, don't do that. Don't build this up. I need you to be the smart older sister you've always been because I have two courses of action and I need you to help me make the intelligent choice."

"I will. I'm just saying you've always sold yourself short when it comes to guys. Tell me your options as you see them. Maybe I'll have another one for you," Beckett said with a smile.

"Search for his flaws, fall out of love with him and walk away a stronger woman who's finally over him," she said.

"Okay. That's one. What's the other one?"

"Make him fall in love with me," she said. "But I have no idea how and frankly since he hadn't realized I was a woman until he kissed me...I'm not sure that's viable. Which is sort of why I texted you but now that I've said it out loud, I'm not sure."

"I like option two. I think we can make that work. I mean either way you're taking a huge risk, but you know what Daddy always says..."

"You know how it goes: first your money and then your clothes?" she quipped, using one of their father's famous sayings.

"Well, yeah, but I was thinking more no guts, no glory," Beckett said.

She was too. This was it. Her last chance to make things work with Ollie and she didn't want to blow it. "So can you help me?"

"Girl, you know it. Let me grab my laptop—we are going to need some mood boards for me to do this properly."

"Beckett—"

"You asked for my advice. Let me do this. Oh, let me see the ring before we get started."

She held her hand up to the camera and her sister caught her breath. It really was a stunning ring.

"He said it reminded him of the stars that were in the sky when we had gone for a ride last fall."

"Dang, girl, we might be working with more than I thought."

OLLIE WORKED WITH the new bull riders for a couple of hours and then realized he should text his parents and let them know he was engaged. A part of him wanted to just spring it on them at the Boots & Bangles event that was coming up the following weekend. But his mom would have women possibly waiting for him to date and he didn't want to let them down. It was a huge fundraiser in Whiskey River. Though his family had only moved there a year earlier, they were already totally integrated into the community. Angelica, his younger sister, had opened her boutique on the Square, his oldest brother Jock—the TV celebrity chef—had opened a restaurant in neighboring Last Stand. Nico was currently living between New York and Whiskey River with his fiancée—Cressida Cormac, the famed luxury basket weaver who had been profiled in *Oprah* magazine and in many up-market shops. His mom had joined the Women of Whiskey River and his father had opened an office for Rossi Import/Export downtown, but his parents were hopeful he'd give up the rodeo and take over running the family business from his father.

No matter how many times he'd told them no, they still held out hope. And an engagement to Colby would go a long way to convincing them he was serious. She wasn't a local girl. Her life was on the road like his. And though her family lived in Georgetown, he wasn't sure where she wanted to settle down if she ever did. He was content living on the road. But he was thirty. Not that the number meant much to him, but he knew he was getting to an age where he was going to have to figure out what he wanted for the rest of his life.

His pops had pulled him aside over Christmas and mentioned that the time for going where the wind took him was over. Which had simply made Olivier more determined to keep on the road. He was the youngest son, not the spoiled apple of his father's eye that his baby sister was. He was the troubled one who no one knew what to do with.

And he liked it that way.

But he was tired of the side conversations from everyone including his brothers who were both always saying *let's get a drink* and then talking up the good points of living in one town.

Colby wasn't going to do anything but show them he was settled in one part of his life, that perhaps having a partner would reassure them he had a plan.

And the fact that his plan was to fool them into thinking he had direction, made him realize how ridiculous he was. He didn't want anyone worrying about him and he was tired of being set up with decent women whom he had no intention of settling down with. His mom had no idea what his type was…

In fact, until today he would have said he didn't have a type.

But now he was seeing long brown hair, big brown eyes

and that kissable mouth of Colby's. Now he knew exactly the type of woman he wanted. Which made no sense since she was his buddy. Not some easy-come-easy-go girl. But there was no denying that he wanted her. He had thought of her several times this afternoon, the way her perfume smelled like spring and the way her braid had lain against her shoulder.

He shook his head. This wasn't helping. He needed to get his head together. He'd made her a promise. One he intended to keep. They were doing this from March to June—that was it. No longer. He couldn't start fantasizing about taking her to his bed. Because as she said they weren't intending to stop being friends—

Hold up.

She hadn't said that. She'd said unless one of them was quitting the rodeo they shouldn't publicize it here. She knew that coming back to work after June was going to be a challenge if they didn't stick to the deal.

Fake fiancée.

That meant no more kissing her and pulling her into his arms, cupping that sweet, perfect ass of hers and rubbing his throbbing erection against her. He groaned. Just the thought of that embrace had him hardening.

This wasn't helping.

He had to figure out how to keep her as she'd always been. It was probably just him being romantic and because of the ring and the proposal. The next time he saw her things would be back to normal.

It was a hot kiss, but just one kiss. He'd never struggled to control his desires and doubted that he would have that problem now. Colby meant too much to him as a friend. He didn't want to fuck it up.

He would wait and introduce her when they got to Whiskey River for Boots & Bangles. That would give him time to feel more comfortable with Colby and for her to be comfortable with him. But he did text his mom to say he was bringing a date to the dance so she wouldn't have one ready for him. Since it was a charity event everyone who attended booked a table in advance. Because his family was so big, they had a round of ten reserved.

His mom texted back a smiling face emoji with heart eyes. *Can't wait to meet her.*

He just hearted her message and then put his phone away. There, it was done. He was committed to this idea. As if he was going to change his mind now after he'd changed everything with Colby.

COLBY HAD TALKED to her sister for over two hours the previous day. She'd gone to practice in the morning and talked to young girls who were thinking of pursuing a career as barrel racers, which made her think again about something that Ollie had mentioned. Coaching. She'd never thought about when she'd stop following the rodeo circuit. She liked it to be honest but talking to Beckett yesterday had made her realize how much she also missed home.

She talked to the girls about cutting around the barrel and the techniques that she'd learned when she was younger. They were between the ages of ten and twelve, she thought. She gave them tips on how to hold their reins and signed some pictures that they had brought along with them. She posed for a photo with them, along with her horse and Shep. Attention hog that he was, he'd trotted over to the girls and sat between them until the girls had petted him while Colby had been riding.

Seeing those girls had stirred something inside of her. Something sort of maternal and that she'd never considered before. But being engaged—even fake engaged—was making her think about weddings. Beckett had told her that she should talk about weddings and houses and the like with Ollie to get him thinking of those things.

A part of her was pretty darned sure if she did that, he'd take off running as far away from her as he could get. But thinking about it the night before, she realized she was falling victim to Beckett's plan for Ollie.

Beckett had also warned her that if she wasn't going to lie to Ollie's family then she better make sure they believed in the engagement. Beckett had already promised to be her matron of honor and helped her set up a website for their engagement, which she hadn't made live. She had to talk to Ollie and see if this made him change his mind. Beckett suggested to keep checking in and offering him an out. The more he committed to, Beckett believed, the more likely it was that he wanted to be engaged for real.

She walked her horse back to the stables and cleaned her, fed and watered her before whistling for Shep who didn't come. He'd probably found some more kids who were petting him but when she stepped out of the barn, she saw he was sitting at Ollie's feet as he was texting on his phone. She walked over to him, putting her hands in the back pockets of her jeans.

Be cool.

"Hey."

"Hey. Give me a sec," he said. Finishing up his text and pocketing his phone. "Sorry about that. How are you this morning?"

"Good. Had a nice practice with horse. I think this is going to be a good weekend."

"Me too. The new riders are hungry but smart," he said. "So I let my mom know I was bringing a date but didn't mention the engagement because I didn't want you to have to deal with that yet."

"Thanks for that," she said. "Um, my sister recommended that we create an engagement website so your family will have a place to learn about us."

"You told your sister?"

"Yeah. I told her the truth by the way," she said. "I didn't want to lie to her, and I want to make this look real."

She hadn't meant to tell him about Beckett but to be fair Colby had never been good at lying. The one time she'd gone out with friends to the lake and drank a beer, she'd broken out in a cold sweat when her daddy had asked her what she'd done at the lake with them. Which had of course given her away.

"That makes sense. The website is a good idea too. I mean I didn't know that was a thing. What else did she mention?" he asked.

Okay, this is it. She smiled at him and just forgot about pretend. "She suggested we talk about the type of wedding we want to have since people will ask. Also, where we see ourselves living. Normally I go to my parents during the off-season, but I can't do that with a husband...or could I?"

He shoved his hands through his hair, musing over it as he tipped his head back. "These are all good things to discuss. This is way more complicated than I'd anticipated. Do you have any ideas?"

"I do. Want to go grab some lunch and I'll show you? I want this to feel like you and me, so if I have anything you don't like speak up," she said.

She figured that this was her chance to show Ollie what life with her would be like. He already knew the rodeo stuff but that was just one part of the woman she was. Beckett said to start acting like he was her boyfriend, treat him the way she wanted him to treat her.

It was harder than she thought it would be because she

had to let down her guard. And she was already so vulnerable to him. But no guts, not glory, right?

"Sounds good."

"I'll meet you at my truck. I need to feed Shep and get him in the trailer and then we can go. I'll bring my tablet so I can show you the website stuff I did. Also, we should try to take some selfies."

He pulled her into his side and took his phone out and snapped a photo. She looked up at him and was smiling, she noted as he handed her the phone.

"We look like a real couple."

She nodded. They did. He was looking down at her with a rapturous look on his face. She could only hope that he'd start feeling like that toward her for real. She was determined to give this everything she had. Hopefully before the end of June he would be.

Chapter Four

OLIVIER HAD BEEN told numerous times that his mouth wrote checks his body couldn't cash and for the most part, he lived to prove the naysayers wrong, but as he sat across from Colby looking into her deep brown eyes, something in the pit of his stomach said this time he might have.

She had a notebook next to her on the table and was sipping her sweet tea while she tried to connect to the restaurant Wi-Fi so she could show him the engagement website she'd created for them.

Christ.

He'd definitely bitten off way more than he'd expected with this. It was supposed to be two friends helping each other out.

But as she tapped on the screen, typing in the password, he realized again how beautiful she was. Like how had he missed that in all the years they'd been friends?

He knew part of it was that the rodeo was his home and his family. Sure, he was a Rossi, but this was where he really felt at home. He could let down all the outside expectation and just be himself. So he hadn't wanted to ever ruin this for himself.

Had he?

Had asking Colby to be his fake fiancée signaled the death knell for this idyllic life he'd had for the last five years?

He hoped not.

He wasn't sure how much longer his body was going to be able to handle the bumps, breaks and bruises that came from being a rodeo cowboy but on the other hand he had no idea what he wanted for the future.

He wasn't like Jock, the celebrity chef; or like Nico, the Wall Street whiz. He was just Ollie. In his family he was the underachiever and the one everyone worried about. Even his sister, Angelica, had two boutiques and a thriving business.

"What do you think?"

"Huh?"

"Are you okay?" she asked. "Seems like you're not really all here."

She reached across the table, putting her hand over his and a shot of pure desire went through him. Right up his arm, down his chest and hardening his groin. Unexpected but totally unwelcome.

This is Colby, he reminded himself as he pulled his hand back.

"Sorry. Was just thinking about family things. Show me the website," he said.

"Well, I wasn't sure what to put in the message or our story. I mean I figured we'd say something like we met in the rodeo. I saw one site where a barrel racer claimed her fiancé was fast but not faster than her because she caught him. But that's not really me and I don't think you either."

He rubbed the back of his neck, realizing that this lie was taking on a shape of its own. "I didn't mean to do any of this."

She pulled her hands back and put them in her lap. "Is it too much? I'm not sure how to be a fake fiancée, Ollie."

No she didn't. In fact, she had a hard time lying. He knew that about her. It was one of the things that he liked about her. But this...he didn't want her to forget this was just for a few months. Just to get through Nico's wedding and then...well then, they'd go back to being friends.

"I don't know about any of this either. I'm just...I don't want either of us to get hurt. This is temporary—don't forget that."

She pursed her lips and tipped her head to the side. A sweep of bangs fell over her forehead as she took a deep breath. "Why would I forget it?"

"I don't know. Just this feels a little too real."

"It has to look real or else I'll look like a fool. I'm not going to visit your family and pretend we're engaged when everyone can see we aren't. Tell me you understand that," she said.

How could he not? She was mad—he could see it in the controlled way she was handling herself. She was his friend. He had to make this right because he'd never wanted to put her in this kind of position.

"Yes, I get it. Show me the website. I'll write the stuff for the site," he said. "I have a Masters of Fine Arts in studio arts and there was a huge research and writing component."

"What?"

He could see he'd shocked her. Part of the reason he'd ended up as a rodeo cowboy was that fine arts was a difficult thing to make a career out of. And he didn't want to set himself up with that kind of pressure.

"Yeah, my parents insisted I go to college during the off-season. They keep hoping I'll find something other than cowboying as a career."

"Why didn't you ever say?" she asked.

Why hadn't he? Well hell, he knew that was because he had wanted her to simply see him as Ollie. He had kept that part of himself private so there was no expectation that he was anything more than she saw here. A small-time rodeo clown with a penchant for one-night stands.

Had he been trying to fool himself or her? Did he think that would make her like him in a different way? He knew he had. He hadn't wanted the dynamic between them to be altered and then he'd gone ahead and kissed her. The fake fiancée thing was way easier to handle than that kiss had been.

"Because it's something I had to do for them. My family are all massive overachievers and I'm a rodeo clown. When I'm home the pressure to step up is intense and so I just keep going back to school. At least it looks like I'm trying and good thing I've done that because I can write the stuff we need for this website."

"What of art do you do?" she asked.

"Oil on canvas mostly—usually rodeo folks or people I see in the stands," he said, realizing that he never talked about this with anyone.

"That's great. Have you thought about doing a show?"

"I have, but success scares me. Something happens to me when I get too close to what I want and I have this destructive side that kicks in," he admitted.

"Is that why you're a rodeo clown?" she asked.

"Partially. I love the thrill of it, you know. I love the excitement of it. I also like the small community we have here, like you I'm sure."

"I do like that. I mean I know I'm aging out of being competitive and a part of me is starting to think of settling down but at the same time...I don't want to give this up," she admitted.

"Me either," he said, realizing for the first time that part of the reason was Colby. If he stopped rodeoing, he wouldn't see her every day.

She put her hand on his again. That same pulse went through him as she rubbed her thumb over his knuckles. "I had no idea you were an artist. We will make this engagement look real and get them off your back temporarily. If you want them to be satisfied for good, you're going to have find a real woman to marry."

"Nah," he said. "These photos are good. When did you get me in the pen?"

"Last season. That bull…he wanted you and I was so scared you weren't going to roll into the barrel in time, so I started taking pictures. It's a nice distraction," she said.

He turned his hand over hers, lacing their fingers together. And though he knew he shouldn't he leaned across the table; their eyes met.

"You were scared for me?"

She nodded. "I always am. You take chances no one else would—that's why the crowd loves you so much—but sometimes I can't breathe."

Her words wrapped around him, sharpening his desire to kiss her. He wanted her. He hadn't meant to but the more they talked like this…it made him realize that asking her to be his fiancée was going to be way trickier than any bull he'd ever faced.

COLBY DIDN'T NEED to hear about Ollie's home life to make her like him more, but she loved these little details that he suddenly was sharing with her. She refused to let herself think that this gamble she was taking might not pay off. She just wasn't going to do it.

When she had started barrel racing no one had thought she had the strength or the skills to be good at it. But she'd never let that deter her. She lived to prove others wrong and show herself that she was right. This time though, she might have bitten off more than she could chew.

As Ollie looked into her eyes, she could smell that spicy, one-of-a-kind aftershave that he wore. That electric-blue gaze of his making her believe he could see all the way to her soul. That the game she was playing, to try to win him as her own, was going to be totally visible.

She'd never been this unsure of anything. But she'd loved Ollie for too long not to take the risk.

Right?

Or was this just one more lie she was telling herself?

"I got beef brisket and pulled pork. Which one of y'all has which?" the waitress asked, breaking the spell that Ollie had put her under.

Colby pulled her hands back and smiled up at the waitress. "I'm the pulled pork and he's the brisket."

She set their plates down and then noticed the image on the tablet. "Are y'all engaged?"

Colby swallowed hard, looking over at Ollie who winked at her and then turned to the waitress. "We are. We haven't had a chance to tell anyone yet. So you're the first person to know."

"Well, congrats. Dessert is on me. Y'all are a cute couple," she said as she turned and walked away.

A cute couple.

That was a start.

"There we go. That went well," Ollie said. "And we got dessert out of it."

"Olivier Rossi, don't get cocky. That woman doesn't even know us. She'd be surprised if we were lying to her."

"The dessert here is pretty good," he said.

She shook her head and then nodded. "It is. But still…we can afford $5.99."

"We certainly can," he said. "How did you think my announcement went? I wasn't kidding about it being the first time I've said we're engaged."

"I know. I think it went well. You sounded a bit nervous and sort of excited," she said—reminding herself that while that reaction was one she wanted to see in him, she knew he hadn't fallen for her between the time they'd entered the booth and their food had been delivered.

"Good. Next time I think we should hold hands. Makes us seem like we are really in love."

Humph.

"What was that?"

"Hold hands…is that what you'd do if you loved me?" she asked.

Then warned herself to be careful; she was treading on thin ice here. She was pushing too hard for what she wanted and probably overplaying her hand.

"I'm not sure what I'd do, but holding hands seems like a nice way to say we are together in this new adventure," he said, picking up his fork and starting to eat.

"It certainly does," she said. She started eating too and they talked about the website as they did. Their waitress cleared their lunch plates and brought them back dessert and insisted on taking a photo of them.

Which Colby thought was nice until Ollie came over to her side of the booth and pulled her into his arms to pose for the photo. His body was pressed all along her left side. He turned his face toward hers and their noses touched and then she felt the brush of his warm breath against her lips. She saw his pupils dilate and for a minute she thought he was going to kiss her in this barbecue restaurant with their waitress watching them. But instead, he just smiled at her and slid out of the booth as the waitress said she was done and put Colby's phone back on the table.

Colby's hands were shaking so she linked them together instead of reaching for her phone. She wanted...that kiss. She needed that kiss. And she thought that Ollie did too. Did this mean her plan was working?

She didn't want to analyze it.

"Let's see the photo," he said.

She picked up her phone and clicked on it. They were both staring into each other's eyes, a sort of smile on Ollie's face. Her own...well in her expression she saw that deer in the headlights look that mirrored the feeling deep in her gut. Like she was afraid he'd read the truth in her eyes.

She scrolled through the photos the waitress had taken. She'd gotten more than one. The first one looked okay. She selected it and then handed it back to Ollie.

"Not bad," she said. "This lunch was really productive. I mean we have the website sorted and we can go ahead and wrap this up until we go to that thing in Whiskey River."

She was talking too much and too fast but she was nervous and it wasn't getting any easier to hope he didn't scroll through the photos but he was. She saw his finger swiping and then he stopped.

"I like this one," he said. "It looks like we both can't wait another moment to be alone."

She took the phone and swallowed as she realized how true his words were. But he thought she was faking. "Does it? We're both in character I guess."

"I guess," he said.

They ate their dessert with a sort of quiet between them and she wondered what he was thinking but was too busy trying to marshal her own thoughts and get her act together. She wanted him to fall for her. Not realize she loved him and run for the hills. She needed to be careful.

COLBY HAD PRACTICE when they returned to the rodeo site and left him without a backward glance. It was odd to be working on a website for their engagement and maintaining this real part of their lives at the rodeo. He definitely didn't blame Colby for insisting that no one who was part of this world know the truth. It was odd enough balancing both in his head.

What would the consequences be if someone found out? He wasn't sure. He didn't mind everyone knowing they were engaged. But if they faked it and then broke up, Colby might face some fallout.

The rodeo was still pretty alpha male with their attitudes so he guessed he'd get a lot of "attaboy" and Colby would get the side-eye and speculation. Which just pissed him off. And that made him realize that he couldn't act on the attraction he felt for her.

He'd danced around trying to justify it in his mind. It would definitely add an element of realism to their fake engagement, but the cost would be too high. He hadn't considered he might be doing irreparable damage to his friendship with Colby. If someone in their small rodeo family cottoned on to the fact that they were lovers...well it would be like he'd just realized.

He needed to treat her like he did his sister. Except he'd never seen Colby as a sister. He's always seen her more as a friend who he could let his guard down and be himself with. And now he was going to have to put his guard up. He couldn't let on that he wanted her, that he wanted to take their relationship to a physical level.

But damn, he thought as he shoved his hands through his thick hair. He wanted her.

So badly.

"Dude, you look like someone just killed your horse."

He opened his eyes and saw that Nicholas Blue was standing next to him. He'd met the stock provider in Whiskey River this past Christmas. It had been nice to finally meet the legend that was the former bull-riding champ. Nick lived in Whiskey River with his wife Reba and their toddler Martina.

"Nah."

"Oh…so a woman?"

He gave a wry laugh. "How'd you guess?"

"Only two reasons why a man looks like you do, and you said your horse was fine," Nick said. "It's too late for me to head home. You working tonight?"

Ollie shook his head.

"Great. Want to join me for a beer or two? I hate being away from my girls, but it'd be nice to have some masculine conversation."

Ollie laughed. "Sure. I got a case back at my trailer unless you want to go to town?"

"Lead on."

Ollie led the way to his trailer. He got beers for himself and Nick. Shep, Colby's dog, whined inside her trailer. "I'll be back."

"Take your time. I'm going to text my girls," Nick said.

Ollie let himself into Colby's trailer and Shep rushed to greet him and then headed to the door. He let the dog out, knowing that Colby wouldn't mind. That was part of the reason that they'd become friends in the first place. She needed someone to keep an ear out for Shep while she was riding.

The dog did his business and then Ollie cleaned up and led him back to his own campsite. He poured some water into the bowl he kept outside for Shep but the animal just curled up next to his chair. Ollie sat down and took a swallow of his beer.

"Who's this?" Nick asked after he finished with his phone.

"Shep. He belongs to a barrel racer."

"My wife used to barrel race," Nick said. "They are usually pretty feisty."

He wasn't sure where Nick was going with this but given that the guy had already guessed that he had a woman on his mind, it seemed like he was just leaving an opening in case he wanted to talk.

Except since his situation was fucked up, the last thing that Ollie wanted to do was discuss it. Also there was a pretty good chance that Nick would be at the Boots & Bangles event given that he and his brothers were bigwigs in town.

"Yeah, they are," he said. "You going to Boots & Bangles?"

"F—. Yes. But I left home so I didn't have to talk about that damned event. All the wives are talking about dresses and getting donations for the silent auction."

Ollie laughed. "I get it. My mom and sister just joined the Women of Whiskey River and have been texting me requests and suggestions for the event."

"The women live for events like this," Nick said. "And it is nice to get duded up for the night. Reba is a killer when she dresses up."

"Did y'all meet at the rodeo?"

"Yeah. She was friends with me and my friend, Marty... He got killed after being thrown."

He knew the story of Marty Powell. His younger brother Gage had won the pro title a few years ago. Kind of adding a new chapter to the bull-riding family story. "Sorry you lost your friend."

"Thanks. I still ain't over it. But most of the time now the memories are just good ones. You lose anyone?"

Ollie had been lucky in that regard. "No. But I've had a few near misses. I know it's a near thing every time I get in the ring, but damn if I can stop myself from doing it."

"Same. I mean even after Marty...I still miss it. But Reba would neuter me if I even thought of going back in."

He laughed. "I can't wait to meet your wife."

"Yeah, she's a pistol. You coming back for Boots & Bangles? That why you were asking about it?"

"Yeah. I went to the Harwood function at Christmas...stag, but my mom had like three single women lined up for me to meet."

Nick laughed and shook his head. "Need a fix-up before you come?"

"No, he doesn't."

He turned to see Colby standing there. She had her straw cowboy hat in one hand and a water bottle in the other. "I'll be with him."

"She sure will be," Ollie said standing up. "Nicholas Blue, meet Colby, my fiancée."

"Pleased to meet you, ma'am."

Chapter Five

COLBY WAS TIRED. She'd been distracted when she'd been running the barrels and her times had reflected that. In one day, her entire focus had switched, and she was lost. Adrift. She'd come back from the winter break with a clear objective—get over Ollie. And all he'd done was look at her with his sexy, puppy dog eyes, asked her to be his fake fiancée and she'd forgotten about her own goals.

She'd folded like a house of cards and honestly at this moment she wasn't sure if that was a good thing or bad. She knew that her sister would say it was good. That maybe the fact she'd given in so easily meant that she'd picked the thing she really wanted.

And of course, that was right.

She wanted Ollie.

But not like this. They were starting a relationship with a big-ass lie. In her heart she knew this was wrong. That she was taking scraps from him and pretending it was a T-bone dinner. But she knew it wasn't.

So she had to be very careful not to lie to herself.

Her heart was racing as she came around the corner and

caught a glimpse of Ollie sitting in a lounge chair, petting Shep's head as he talked. His voice was a sexy deep rumble that made her remember that moment at lunch when she'd forgotten everything and they'd almost kissed.

Nothing had felt fake.

Nothing.

Which was probably why she was doing this.

She didn't recognize the guy he was talking to. She heard him mention setting Ollie up and she knew why she'd put aside her own safety to take this risk. She saw red. There was no need to set Ollie up with any other woman. He had her. She was going to show him that he never needed another woman.

She put her hand on his shoulder and owned the fiancée thing even here on her home turf. If she had a shot in hell of winning him over and making him fall in love with her, she was going to have to be his fiancée everywhere. And she had to stop thinking fake. She wanted this to be real. If they acted engaged in their real lives then maybe Ollie would start to fall for her.

Now she was sitting around the campfire with Nicholas Blue and Ollie, and it was easy to forget that she and Ollie weren't a real couple. Nick was funny and easy to talk to. He was a bit of a flirt and a charmer, but he was also clearly in love with his wife and daughter. No lie, Colby had seen no less than twenty photos of both of them over the course of the evening.

"Reba is going to like you, Colby. Y'all have to stay an extra day or two in Whiskey River so we can have you to our place," Nick said as he was getting ready to leave.

"We'll see," Colby said. "Depends on the rodeo schedule."

"Fair enough," Nick said, waving goodbye as he left.

Ollie turned to her where they were seated in their camp chairs. "Would you really stay an extra day there?"

"Yeah. If you wanted to. I liked Nick. His family sounds nice," she said.

"Yeah…"

She could tell something was bothering him and a part of her wanted to ignore it. Like she had all the other times in the past. But she was trying to make this real, so she shoved her own nerves aside. "What's the matter?"

He did that thing where he rubbed his hand over the top of his head. Then took a deep swallow of his beer before settling back in his chair and kicking his legs out in front of him. "I'm not sure we should have couple friends."

"Why not? You're the one who is trying to fool his parents," she said. She was tired of him seeming to go back and forth on this. "This was your idea. Us doing couple things together will definitely make your mom believe this is real."

"Cool your horses, cowgirl. I'm just trying to figure this out. It's clear I had no idea what this would entail when I asked you," he said. "I know most of the time I seem like I'm the smartest thing—"

She snorted.

"Hey!"

"Sorry. But you seem like you are savvy and good at getting what you want. I'm not sure that translates to smarts."

"Fair enough," he said.

She didn't know if it was the fire weaving its magic in the night or just some of the new bravado she'd been channeling but... "What did you want when you asked me to do this?"

Ugh.

As soon as the words left her mouth, she wanted to call them back, but she was in now. She wasn't going to back down. She turned so she could more fully meet his gaze. She needed to know the truth of this.

He shrugged before finishing his beer in a long swallow. "I guess...I wanted you at my side."

Honestly she stopped listening at him saying he wanted her. But the practical part of herself forced her to acknowledge the rest of his sentence. She had to believe in herself. She couldn't compromise that to try to get him to love her.

"Why?"

He leaned over closer to her and she felt that magic from the fire and the night sky dancing all around them. It was just like the moment they'd almost kissed at lunch. She leaned toward him.

He watched her and she felt deep in her gut that this time he was going to be honest with her. Tell her what he really wanted from her.

"I figured it would be more fun to have you by my side," he said.

Oh.

She sat back and snapped her fingers for Shep. She'd had enough of this. She needed to sleep and get a clear head.

"I'm sure it will be tons of fun," she said as she stood and walked away from the fire and its false magic, but more importantly from Ollie and his dreamy eyes that were making her believe in something that had never been there.

OLLIE KNEW HE'D said the wrong thing, but lines were getting blurred, and he wasn't entirely sure that after having drunk about six beers that he was in the best state of mind to be discussing Whiskey River, his family and the woman that he was slowly realizing he wanted as more than a friend.

She was mad.

He should let her go.

He couldn't.

He followed her, stopping her with his hand on her arm. She turned and he saw more than anger on her face; she was upset too.

"Cowgirl—"

"Don't. Please. If you value our friendship—"

"But I do, Colby-girl. I value it so much more than you'll ever know, which is why I have to make this right," he said. "I'm not worried about making friends for any reason other than I think it might blur the lines between us. Maybe I'll start thinking you're more than my best friend and kiss you again…"

Her lips parted and she sort of sigh-gasped. "Would that be so bad?"

"Wouldn't it?" he countered.

But the sky was big and filled with stars or maybe satellites and the moon was full, and it felt like maybe there weren't too many consequences. Like maybe for once he could just reach out and grab what he wanted instead of following the role he'd assigned himself years ago. The rambling cowboy, the good-time guy.

She turned so that she was more fully facing him, and her body was only a scant few inches from his. He looked down into her upturned face and he knew there was no way he was walking away from her unscathed. There was too much to like about Colby even before he'd kissed her. Now it was all he could do to keep from throwing her over his shoulder and taking her to bed.

He groaned. Images in his mind of her riding him the way she did her horse as she barreled at full speed. He could see her hair flying around her shoulders, her breasts bobbing—

"Ollie, I don't know," she admitted. "I think I'm waiting for a signal but I'm not sure what it is."

A signal…for what?

Oh, if they should let this become real.

He reeled in his lust as best he could. He had to man up. That was another layer to the role he'd cast himself in here. "Yeah, I know what you mean. I want you, Colby. I'm not going to lie about that. When I kissed you…well it changed things. I'm not sure I can go back to what we had before."

She put her hand on his jaw, sort of cupping the side of his face. "Me either. I just can't figure out if that's good or bad."

"Something in my jeans is telling me it'd be real good."

She looked down, spotted his erection and then looked back up. "Um. Okay. Well, I'm not—"

"I know you're not ready for that. I'm just saying being around you, Colby-girl, turns me on. It used to just be your laughter I wanted and some fiery debate about whatever topic we talked about, but now it's more."

"More," she said. Then she shook her head. "I sound like a damn parrot. You've rattled me."

He couldn't help but smile at that. She was tough. Cowgirl tough and could handle anything that the world threw at her. It was hard for him to see this as a bad thing.

"I'm glad."

"Brat."

"You know it. I don't want to say let's see what happens," he admitted.

She tipped her head to the side and that cascade of her bangs fell against her forehead. He reached up and pushed it back away from her eyes.

"Why not?"

"Because you're you."

Even as he said it, he realized that it sounded cheesy and maybe like a cop-out, but he meant it. Any other woman…well, he would have hustled her into his bed and when he brought her home, his mom would know he wasn't really engaged. But this was Colby. She'd been different from the moment he'd met her and now…well he'd changed the dynamics. He'd done this. So it was up to him to make sure she didn't get hurt and he didn't take advantage of this.

Of her.

"I'm me?"

He just smiled and nodded.

"How many beers did you drink?"

Not enough. Not nearly enough to dull his senses or his wits where she was concerned. It had just made him more aware of her and more aware of how much he didn't want to screw this up.

"A fair few," he said. "But not too many. I have the qualifying to work tomorrow."

She caught her breath and he remembered what she'd mentioned about taking pictures because it distracted her.

"You know you don't have to watch me in the ring," he said.

"I know. I like to. It's exciting and you're funny and so good at what you do," she said. "I wouldn't miss it."

"I'm glad. I like knowing you are out there watching me," he admitted. Shep came back and nudged their legs and he noticed Colby shiver from the cool evening air.

"I better let you get to bed."

"Instead of taking me to yours."

He realized her mind and his were on the same page. But they had both hesitated and he'd already decided to do the gentlemanly thing. But he needed something. He pulled her into his arms and lowered his head. Took the long deep kiss his body demanded and then groaned when her tongue brushed over his and he knew he wasn't going to have an easy time of letting go of her.

She had her arms around his shoulders, holding him to her as she leaned into him.

THE FEEL OF his lips against her was quieting every objection she could think of and to be honest there weren't that many. He was afraid he'd fall for her. It seemed like that was the very thing she wanted, yet a part of her knew there was a chance he wouldn't and then where would she be?

But his kiss.

Damn.

She had dreamed of what this would be like, but the feel of his hands on her back, sliding down to cup her butt and pull her more fully into his body as he kissed her... She hadn't been even close to realizing what that would feel like or what it would do to her.

His erection was hard and thick between them. She heard him groan as his hips rocked against her and she shifted her stance, lifting her leg slightly around his thigh so that his shaft rubbed against her center. She melted.

Her legs went a little bit weak, and she knew that she wasn't going to pull away from him or step back from this moment.

But then Shep barked and took off after something. She turned her head and heard the sound of a scuffle.

"Shep," she yelled.

"I'll get him," Ollie said as he ran after her dog. There were wild animals out here. She was always careful to keep Shep in at night. The last time he'd scuffled like this she'd had to take him to the vet for stiches.

She heard Ollie's sharp yell for Shep and then the sound of him scaring off the other animal. Both of them were back a moment later. Her pulse was racing, and she fell to her knees to greet her dog. Shep wasn't too roughed up. "Bad dog. Don't do that again."

She opened the door to her trailer, and he hopped up inside before looking back at Ollie and then he disappeared toward his bed. She closed the door and looked over at Ollie.

His hair was mussed, his face hard with worry. He put his hands on his hips, drawing her gaze down his body. He was still turned on. She was too, but tonight wasn't the night for sex.

"You didn't sound strict enough when you scolded him," he said.

"I didn't?"

"No."

"Sorry but it's hard to yell at him for following his instincts and when I wasn't paying attention to him." She closed the distance between the two of them. "Thank you for going after him and for caring about him."

He shook his head and rubbed his hand over his chest. "You don't have to thank me. He's a good dog. And you're right—he was just following his instincts."

They had been too. "Seems to be the night for that."

He gave a chuckle and nodded. "It certainly does. That kiss…I'm going to do it again unless you ask me not to."

A shiver went through her and she felt herself get wet. "Tonight?"

"No, not tonight, but soon," he said.

"Good."

"Good? Damn, Colby-girl, how am I supposed to be smart about this when…you aren't making it easy?"

"Am I making it hard again?" she asked. Realizing that she finally felt free to flirt with him. She'd been hiding this part of herself from him for too long. She liked it. She liked his reaction. The surprise on his face at first.

He wriggled his eyebrows at her. "Yeah, you are. And I've already promised you that I would keep my hands to myself tonight."

"Yeah you did," she said. "But I didn't make any promises."

He groaned. "If you touch me, all bets are off. I wouldn't have any regrets, would you?"

Regrets? She had a million of them. She wanted him. She felt achy and empty just standing across from him. But she knew if this didn't play out the right way she was going to end up with one night in his arms and a lifetime of looking back. She wanted to do it right. She was trying to make him fall in love with her. Lust was a good way to start.

"I'm not sure, so I think that has to be the answer, right?"

He nodded and then reached over to cup the side of her face and rubbed his thumb over her lips, which sent another shiver through her, making her almost change her mind.

"Good night, Colby-girl. Sleep tight and dream of me."

She'd have no problem doing that.

"You too," she said, turning and walking to her trailer. She knew he was watching her so she took her time, very aware of the sway of her own hips, and when she let herself into the trailer she turned to look back at him.

"Night."

He lifted his hand and waved at her. She closed the door and then leaned back against it.

Was this a victory or a stalemate?

She wanted to analyze it and figure him out but at the same time she wanted to just enjoy the fact that he'd kissed her.

Like really kissed her and maybe for a few hours she could forget about fake engagements and make-him-fall-for-her plans.

She threw herself on her bed and stared at the ceiling. To be honest she never would have guessed when he'd entered her trailer yesterday that instead of getting over Ollie Rossi she'd have made out with him.

Dang.

This was so much better than what she'd felt as she'd come back. She'd been waiting years and wondering what he'd feel like in her arms and now she knew. She pulled her pillow to her chest and hugged it. Whatever else happened she had this night. This moment when they'd been a couple and made a new friend and then...

He'd kissed her so long and deep that all the doubts she'd had about trying to make him fall in love with her had disappeared. Her resolve was solidified. Ollie Rossi was going to be her man—not for fake but for real.

Chapter Six

THE RODEO WEEKEND went by in a blur. He had a busy time of it, distracting the bulls and playing to the crowd. Colby won her event but before he had a chance to congratulate her, she'd texted to say her sister had driven in and was taking her to dinner.

He came out of the changing room to see the usual suspects loitering by the door. A fair number of buckle bunnies a few he'd spent the night with last year smiled at him as he came out. He was facing an evening alone and was tempted to take one of them to dinner and see what happened. But that didn't sit well with him. He might only be temporarily engaged to Colby, but he was going to be true to her until the end of June as he'd promised.

He walked on by them and headed not toward his truck but toward his trailer. He got home in time for his family's weekly video call. Sunday dinner had long been a tradition in their family and during the height of the pandemic when they were all scattered around the country—Jock in Last Stand, Nico in Manhattan, and himself at a campground, they'd started doing these weekly video chats.

Mostly they all called in when they could. There was no pressure. Though his mom always said how much she missed seeing all her babies. As a rule, Ollie avoided them. It wasn't that he didn't love his family, he did. It was more that when he was with them, he was always the odd man out. That underachiever whose big dream from childhood was to be a cowboy. His parents and siblings never said anything untoward to him, but he always felt...well, judged.

Still. He hadn't talked to them in a while and tonight he didn't want to be alone. No matter that the pressure of his family was intense at times, some of that was off now that he had Colby.

He dialed in and found that his eldest brother Jock was on the call with his new wife Delilah.

"Baby bro! Good to see you. How was the rodeo?" Jock asked.

"Good to see you both too. It was fine. Some great bulls in the mix. A few close calls but I think the crowd enjoyed it."

"I bet they did," Delilah said. "I saw you last summer in Last Stand and you were impressive."

"I didn't know that," he said. "You should have come over and said hi."

"We didn't know each other then."

"Oh, so it was back when you hated all celebrity chefs?" Jock asked.

"Yes. I mean, I still don't feel that great about all of them so mind yourself," Delilah sassed his brother.

He almost dropped his beer when he realized that was how Colby had been with him last night. That kind of teasing sassiness that women gave a man they liked. He wanted more of it. He knew he wasn't going to be satisfied with keeping his hands to himself for too long. He'd never really had that with a woman—maybe because he kept things light or just sexual. It made him realize how similar he and Colby were to his brother and his sister-in-law.

Whoa.

That wasn't what he wanted. They were doing this thing to get through this summer wedding and his time with his family. He couldn't let the lines blur. What he had with Colby was friendship and a favor. That was it.

"Mom and Dad are running late and heads-up, she's planning to question you about your date for the Boots & Bangles—"

"Great."

"I was sort of surprised you had one," Jock said.

"Yeah, I do date, ya know?"

Delilah laughed and play punched Jock's shoulder. "Idiot."

"Who is she?" Jock asked.

"Colby Tucker."

"The barrel racer?" Delilah asked.

"Yes. Last Stand again?"

"Yeah. That's cool. She's really good," Delilah said.

"She is. She won today, which she does most of the time. She's pretty serious when it comes to riding."

"So you found yourself a cowgirl?"

"Jock, shut it. This is why I don't come on these calls."

"Hey," Jock said, holding up his hands. "I was just asking. Nothing to get upset about. I like the idea of you and a cowgirl. When you were little you always used to say that you and your wife were going to travel the country riding horses all day."

He had forgotten he'd said that, but the truth was back then all he'd wanted to do was ride all day. Luckily Nico popped on before Ollie had to respond.

"Hiya, bros. How's it going?"

"Good." They both said at the same time. Ollie tuned out as his brothers were talking and he heard Cressida in the background and realized that their family calls were becoming a large extended family event.

He liked both Delilah and Cressida but the truth was he sometimes missed the old days of talking shit with his brothers. He waited for his parents and sister to join—they were all together at the Rancho Del Rey in Whiskey River.

His mom gushed with excitement to see all of them together and tried to take a picture of the screen and disconnected them twice before Angelica did it for her.

"Ollie, I mentioned you to a nice girl on the Women of Whiskey River committee in case your date falls through," his mom said toward the end of the call.

"That's nice. She's not going to bale on me," he said.

"Is it serious?" his mom asked.

This was what he'd been building toward. "Yes, it is. I've asked her to marry me."

"What?! Why didn't you lead with that?" his mom asked.

"Congratulations, son," his father said.

His siblings also congratulated him. "What's her name and when can we meet her?"

"Colby Tucker, she's a barrel racer and you can meet her at the gala. I'm not taking a chance on y'all scaring her off before then," he said.

"We're not that bad," his mom said.

"Yes we are," Jock retorted.

His dad chuckled and nodded. They chatted for a few more minutes until the call ended. The first hurdle had been crossed. He was committed to doing this with his family and with Colby. No going back.

Part of him didn't want to.

Another part of him was thinking about the future but that wasn't his concern today. He finished his beer and paced around his camper until he heard Colby's truck pull in. He listened to her letting Shep out before opening the door and stepping outside.

SHE SENSED HIM behind her before he spoke. She had been hoping to avoid this. She had spent the night with her sister getting advice on how to move forward with Ollie, but the truth was she wanted to pretend she didn't need a plan and could just sleep with him. Sleep in his arms and not have any regrets.

The truth was she knew she would. She already had regrets. Last night that she didn't go far enough with that kiss; tonight she wanted to go further but Beckett had said to keep things light. Make him want her but don't give in. That sort of plan made a hell of a lot of sense if she was going to make him fall in love with her. But she was just a girl standing very close to the man she'd wanted and loved for too long and she wanted…

The night sky was again big and clear, the moon still looking full though starting to wane. She turned and looked over her shoulder at Ollie. He had on a close-fitting white T-shirt tucked into a pair of faded Levi's and a thick flannel shirt over it. Unbuttoned. He had one hand in his front pocket.

"Hey."

Hey? Hey. She was so on edge right now and it had everything to do with him. He was so cool and casual and she wasn't. She never had been. She wanted him. She hadn't slept a wink last night thinking about his naked body on tops of hers. She'd raced today to get the fire that was burning in her out and she'd won but she was still empty and aching.

"You okay?" he asked, rubbing his hand on his head like he did.

"No. I'm not okay. I'm trying to be smart about being your temporary fiancée and yet at the same time…we kissed last night and that was real. And I don't know what to do next. My sister said to be cool but let's face it I've never been cool."

"Colby-girl—"

"Don't. Don't sweet-talk me or be kind. Just be blunt and honest. This is ending. You're going to walk away from me at the end of June, right?"

There, she'd said it. She had been trying to pretend that she and Ollie were like some couple in a romantic movie who could fall for each other despite the fact that he'd asked her for a favor. She knew that wasn't the way the real world worked.

She wasn't sure why she'd even considered making him fall for her when the previous five years of knowing her he'd never once—

"I don't know. Yes. I thought we'd pretend to be a couple and then go back to being friends at the end of June," he said. "But now I'm not sure of anything. I'm not going to apologize for kissing you because few things in my life have felt as right as having you in my arms did last night."

She caught her breath, looking over to see if he was just being nice or saying something to appease her. But it didn't look like it. He seemed as torn by the kiss as she did. "So what are we going to do?"

"Well, talking seems like a good thing. I think we need

to both be honest about our feelings. Right now I like the idea of us being a couple. Do you?"

She swallowed and realized that if she went down this road, the truth one, she was going to have to own up to having liked him for a long time. She remembered what Beckett had said, that she should keep that knowledge tucked away until he fell for her. But Colby wasn't like that.

Shep came back from doing his business and she cleaned up after him and then let him back into the trailer, still trying to decide what to say to Ollie. He just waited patiently as if he knew that she wasn't sure.

"I do like that idea," she said at last. "But I know how you are with women. I've seen you date a lot of women."

He moved closer to her. "I have. And it's totally fair of you to be on your guard with me."

Which really told her nothing and made no promises. She suddenly felt tired and foolish. Was she just seeing and hearing what she wanted to with Ollie?

"Did you mean it when you said we had to be honest?"

He stood a little straighter, meeting her gaze squarely. "Yes. You know I'm a man of my word."

She did know that. So this was it. She would ask a tough question and then believe his answer.

"Are you willing to do this for real? Like date and be a real couple? Or is this just something you think will make us look better to your family?" she asked. This was the only thing she could safely ask. She knew there was no way she could ask him if he thought he would fall in love with her. And frankly she wouldn't believe him whatever answer he gave.

"I'm not doing this to make our engagement feel more real. I thought we'd just show up in Whiskey River as a couple and that would be it. When I kissed you, I thought it would be a friendly embrace. I didn't notice you as a woman until that moment."

Well then.

She wanted to be upset by his honesty, but she'd asked for it, and it reassured her in a way that nothing else could have.

"If you're feeling differently, you have to tell me immediately."

"Why?"

"Because I don't have your long experience in casual dating; I'm not sure I can switch it on and off that quickly. I don't want to fall for you if you've already discovered I'm not the one for you."

THE ONE FOR him.

Never in his life had he thought about finding the one. His life was that of a rambler. Which had been underscored tonight by the conversations he'd had—first with his family and second with Colby. She was asking him for the honesty that he'd promised her but at the same time he realized he was going to have to be honest with himself. Was he really interested in Colby? Or was it just the novelty of being with a woman who'd been a good friend to him?

There was no way he could deny that he relied on her friendship in between all the casual hookups he'd had over the years they'd known each other. Now she was asking him to give her a heads-up if his feelings changed.

He'd never been that into feelings where women were concerned. Unless you counted lust and he was pretty sure she didn't. "Sure."

"Sure?"

"You're asking me to identify something I've never thought about before," he said, keeping it as honest as he could.

"What are you talking about? Surely you care about the women you date," she said.

He nodded and then rubbed his hand over his head before dropping his arm. "I like 'em sure but it's not like I really feel anything other than, well, lust and good times. That kind of thing."

She put her hands on her hips and shook her head at him as if he were Shep when he wasn't minding her. "Olivier Rossi, that's the most emotionally stunted thing I've ever heard."

He took umbrage at that. He wasn't stunted. Not at all. "Not everyone has to tell themselves they 'love' the other person to have sex with them."

Her arms dropped to her sides and she gave him a tough, but hurt look. "Is that what you think I do?"

God, how had he let the conversation get to this? He didn't want to talk about his feelings or her feelings or anything like this. But somehow she needed this from him. He was following her lead.

"Yes? Honestly I have no idea."

"Well you're not wrong. I have a hard time letting my guard down with people I don't know. And getting naked never felt like just fun to me. It's always felt like it's leading to something else…"

As soon as she said *naked* he couldn't help but picture her that way, even though she was being so sincere he knew he shouldn't. "It's always just been fun to me. Something to do during the times when I wasn't in the ring."

"Do all guys think that way?"

"I have no idea. This is the most touchy-feely conversation I've ever had. And frankly I'm going to deny it if you mention it to anyone else."

"Why?"

"Because I'm a man. I don't talk about feelings and all that stuff."

"Because you're a man…are you kidding me right now? I saw you cry when Dusty was taken away on a stretcher knowing he was going to be paralyzed and not able to ride again," she said. "You have emotions."

"Hell. Of course I do. I'm not saying I'm a tin man; it's

just I don't talk about them." Of course he had emotions.

"So what emotions do you have when it comes to me?" she asked.

"I like you, Colby-girl, always have. You know that. But now I'm spending a lot of time thinking about you in my arms and how it would have felt to just let things progress last night. But you're talking about emotions and I don't know if I'm the right man for you."

"Why not? You just admitted you have them."

"Having them and talking about them are two different things," he said. "I don't even want to admit to myself what I'm feeling at any given minute."

She walked over to him and put her hand in the center of his chest right over his heart. "How about this? You tell me when something changes...like it did last night when we kissed. I'll do the same."

He thought about that for a minute and tried to figure out what she really wanted from him because he knew she was driving at something.

"What are you afraid of?"

"That once we sleep together, you'll want to go back to just friends, and I will like you more than I do now so your decision will hurt me."

Honesty.

Way more than he'd expected and yet at the same time he wanted to hear it. He needed to try to understand Colby. This Colby. Not the woman he debated books with and talked horses and dogs with.

The Colby who'd kissed his socks off and almost made him come in his jeans. That one was a mystery, and he had no idea what he was doing with her. Or how to move forward in the slightest way.

"I don't want to hurt you," he said, putting his hand on the side of her face to cup her jaw.

Her skin was so soft, but she was so tough. Just his tough cowgirl that could always handle whatever life tossed her way.

"Then don't," she said.

He was going to try his damnedest to make sure that he didn't but now he had to keep in the front of his mind the fact that she was more vulnerable than he'd expected. She never showed any weaknesses and to be fair this wasn't one…well sort of.

He leaned down and kissed her. Not a let's get naked one, but a soft one that he hoped would feel like the promise he wanted to make her. A vow that would keep her safe and happy. Even though he knew he had no power to make that kind of promise.

"Good night," he said.

"Good night, Ollie."

She turned and walked into her trailer and he stood there for a long time in the cool evening air trying to figure out the way forward.

Chapter Seven

COLBY KNEW SHE had to keep herself together. Last night's bout of honesty had just revealed how dangerous this game was she'd started. Probably because it wasn't a game. Not to her. She couldn't make him love her. And she wasn't even sure he'd recognize love if he felt it.

She wasn't sure how to move forward. All the giddy optimism that had been driving her had a sudden impact with reality and it was what she'd been living with for the last five years.

Shep was sitting in the passenger seat of the cab as she drove them to her parents' house in Georgetown. The sun sparkled off her engagement ring, which made her realize that she needed to have her wits about her when they saw her folks. She'd said they would deceive them as well, but the closer she got the less sure she was of it. A glance in the rearview showed that Ollie was a few cars back. This was it, she thought. She needed a sign that she should keep doing this. Dinner with her parents and sister and her family would be a chance for them to be a couple. Should she just be honest with them so she didn't have to be fake engaged but just themselves—Colby and Ollie?

But when she got to her folks' house and parked and Ollie got out of his cab, she realized that she might not be able to lay this down, she might not be able to walk away from him. Even if it was the smart thing to do.

Shep hopped down and ran to do his business near the side of her parents' driveway. They lived on an acreage outside of Georgetown and Shep knew his way around the place.

"Not a bad drive, but I'm glad to be out of the truck," Ollie said as he walked over to her. He had his battered old Stetson on and was watching her the way he'd been when they'd pulled out of the rodeo. Warily.

Last night had definitely changed things and not necessarily for the better. They were both kind of cautious feeling their way now.

"Same. Are you going to take your horse with you to your folks or do you want to stable him here?" she asked. She was leaving hers and Shep with her folks for the weekend, while they went to Whiskey River for the Boots & Bangles gala event.

"Here, I think. I booked us a room at the Harwood House for the weekend. Figured it might be easier for us to have some down time if we needed it from being engaged."

She tipped her head to the side, studying him, trying to see if there was a hidden message in those actions.

"Just in case you needed to chill away from my mom and

sister who are no doubt going to have a lot of questions for you," he said, holding his hands up.

"Thanks," she said.

"Baby girl!"

She turned to see her daddy walking around the side of the house. He held his arms out and she ran to him for a hug. Her dad gave the best hugs and he always made her feel better. "Good to see you."

"You too. Hi there, Ollie," Bert said. Her father had met Ollie numerous times when her parents had come to see her ride.

"Bert," Ollie said. "Thanks for letting us stay the night."

"Like I'd let you two sleep anywhere else. You want to bring the horses back? I had Marshall get a couple of stalls ready."

They both got their horses settled while her father played with Shep and talked Ollie's ear off about Nicholas Blue's bulls. This was the first year that Nick's bulls were old enough to be used in the rodeo. Colby left the men talking, but as she did she realized how naturally Ollie fit in with her family. Well with her dad anyway.

Her mom was in the family room watching her stories. She paused the show to give her a hug. Noticed the ring on her finger and lifted an eyebrow at her. "So Ollie's your…boyfriend now?"

"Yeah." Not sure how her mom was going to react. Was she going to have to try to convince her mom that after five years as friends she and Ollie were now more? She should have thought this through better. Which she hadn't because it was Ollie.

"And the ring?"

"Uh, we're engaged. Sorry I didn't say anything sooner."

"You sound defensive, like that time you broke curfew and went to the lake to drink beer with your friends," her mama said.

"Did you talk to Beckett? She never was good at keeping things quiet," Colby said. In fact it had been her sister who'd told her mom about the beer.

"Yes, I did. She's worried about you and I am too. Is this boy the reason why you never date anyone else?" she asked, patting the spot next to her on the big leather sofa.

Colby glanced behind her to make sure they were still alone and then went into the room and sat next to her mama. "You know he is. He's a man not a boy."

"I know that he's grown, just like your daddy, but that man acts like a boy more often than not."

She smiled as she knew her mom intended but also it made her feel a bit better. Her mom had always known the right thing to say. "I like the idea of the two of you and I think you are doing the only thing you can. You'd regret it if you didn't. I won't tell Daddy."

"Thanks, Mama. We are actually sort of dating…"

"Sort of?" her mom asked with a raised eyebrow. "Does that mean sleeping together?"

"Mama!"

"So not yet," she said.

She shook her head. "The FBI should use you for interrogations."

"They can't afford her," her dad said from the doorway.

Colby turned and saw that Ollie was right behind him. He gave her a quizzical look so maybe he hadn't heard their conversation.

"Hello, Mrs. Tucker."

"Might as well call me Betty now that you two are dating," her mom said. "Good to see you again, Ollie."

"Dating! Boy, why didn't you say so?"

"Thank you, ma'am. I was waiting until Colby and I were together to tell you," Ollie said.

Her parents hugged them both and went out to check on something. Colby suspected her mom was giving her dad the lowdown on her dating Ollie. Ollie came over to her. "That was…how was that for you?"

"Good I guess. You?"

"Yeah. I don't know. I didn't think about how other people would react to us being a couple. Was sort of just focused on my mom. I like your parents so I don't want to disappoint them," he said.

"It was different. But not too bad," she said, realizing that if she wanted Ollie to start thinking of them as a real couple she needed to act like they were. "I sort of like the idea of celebrating us."

"Yeah? Me too," he said, leaning over to kiss her and she closed her eyes as he did so.

This kiss felt...well not for show, but for them and she loved every second of it.

Her dad cleared his throat and they turned to see her folks standing there. They settled into the armchairs to the side. Her parents' housekeeper Pearl came in and said she'd set snacks and her famous peach tea on the back patio by the pool.

Colby and Ollie followed her parents out of the family room and he leaned down. "Everything okay? I get the feeling your mom isn't that keen on you and me."

"She's just cautious," Colby said, wishing she'd inherited a bit of that trait.

OLLIE WAS SLIGHTLY off-balance at the Tuckers house. Her parents were open, friendly, good people, but they were looking at him as their daughter's boyfriend. Things had changed. One more element he hadn't considered when he'd gone to Colby and asked for a favor.

With hindsight he had to wonder if he had known then what he was really asking and how it would impact them all, if he would have asked for the favor. It was hard to say. The truth was he hadn't thought of anything but himself when he'd asked her to help him out.

Her parents didn't know about the entire fake engagement, which was a relief. Colby'd just said they were friends who had started dating or something to that effect. Bert wasn't much of a talker, but he had simply turned to Ollie before they'd come into the house earlier and told Ollie that if he broke Colby's heart he wasn't going to be happy.

Just that.

A few laconic words from the big, gregarious man who was at this moment telling a story about how he'd gotten his truck stuck in the mud on his first date with Betty. It was funny. He was a laidback and easygoing man.

"What was your first date like?" Betty asked.

"Well we went for a ride. Took Shep and a lunch and just rode for a bit," Ollie said.

"It was nice. The weather was great," Colby said.

Her parents looked at the two of them. Ollie wasn't sure that they were selling the first date, but it had been their first date.

"I know it doesn't sound like much," he said. "We sort of headed out as friends, and when we were talking, I realized that Colby was more than a friend."

"I was thinking the same thing," Colby added. "Things just sort of...well, happened. And we both realized we were on the same page."

"Things happened!" Bert said with a loud laugh. "I guess that's the safest way to describe it to your parents."

"Daddy, that's all the detail you're getting."

"Girl, I don't want more than that," he said.

They were all laughing and Ollie finally felt that this favor was the right choice. He had a tight-knit family but Ollie had never let his guard down with them because he was the oddball in the group. Here with the Tuckers, he felt more at home than he wanted to admit.

They played a card game after dinner called BS—bullshit. The game involved a combination of luck and conning of the other players. He enjoyed it and only at the end of the night as Colby won her third hand of the evening, he admitted he hadn't realized that she was so good at lying. Or was she?

Cards weren't life. But he was beginning to realize that she wasn't as gregarious as he'd always thought she was. She'd seemed open, easy to know, and like a guy he'd just taken that at face value.

Her parents went up to bed and Colby showed him to the guest room. But he wasn't tired and not ready to spend another restless night alone without her.

"I heard they were rebroadcasting the rodeo from this weekend. Want to watch it with me?" he asked. "I need to watch the bulls again so I'm ready when we go back."

She nodded. "Yeah. We can use the game room TV," she said. "I want to make some notes on my ride."

"You had about the most perfect ride ever. Everyone was talking about it," he said as he followed her down the hall.

She glanced over her shoulder at him with a smile. "Thanks. But there's always room for improvement."

Not where she was concerned.

The woman was pretty much damned near perfect. Except...except her skills at BS. Was it only cards where she was so good at bluffing or was it life too?

"So how'd you get so good at BS?"

"Mostly because Daddy doesn't think his girls can lie and my mama is always trying to whoop Daddy, so they aren't too focused on what I do."

"I was watching you, and you fooled me too," he admitted.

She winked at him. "That's because you're a man. You were watching me differently. Probably not paying attention to the game."

He narrowed his eyes as he watched her. Had that been true? He had been distracted by her mouth, but hell, he was always distracted by it lately. She just had the kind of mouth that made Ollie want to kiss her.

Which then led to him remembering how well she kissed and the way she tasted. How after they had kissed, he couldn't stop tasting her on his lips. Which had turned him on and...okay, she might have had a point.

"Still...you were pretty darned good."

She just shrugged as she sat down on the leather couch and reached for the remote control. "I was raised to do my best. Always."

"And you do, don't you?"

She chewed her lower lip before tipping her head to the

side. "I try. But this engagement is—"

"Don't think of it that way. I liked us tonight. Let's just do the dating thing and not have the pressure of anything fake."

She took a deep breath and gave him one of her shrewd looks, and he knew she was measuring him and as always with Colby he prayed he wasn't found wanting. But inside he'd judged himself and given himself low scores. Why hadn't he just asked her out instead of setting on this path of temporary engagement and lies?

Nothing good came from lies. He knew that. He'd learned it again and again over the course of his life, but it was a lesson he still didn't seem to have learned.

JUST DO THE dating thing. Colby considered this. "Except you told your parents we're engaged."

"Yeah, I did. What I meant is we don't have to do anything fake for them. Actually I think it will be a lot like dinner with your parents was."

She somehow doubted that. His family was rich. Like had massive amounts of money, houses, success. Things she wasn't used to. His sister Angelica was in a viral video that had shown up on TMZ, all the gossip websites and had her picture splashed across the tabloids.

His eldest brother was Jock Rossi. The celebrity chef of the *Perfect Bite*. His middle brother a brand manager to the rich and famous, navigating social media accounts and big business deals. His family was nothing like her rancher father, and charity worker mother.

"Uh, okay."

"What do you mean by that?" he asked.

"Just that your family have been in magazines and on TV shows. Your family is a lot different than mine."

"Fair enough. But that doesn't make them any different as people than your parents."

She wondered if she'd offended him by pointing out that lifestyles of the rich and famous wasn't what she was used to. Probably. But she was tired and edgy tonight. The day had taken a bigger toll on her emotions than she'd realized.

She wished she could relax and just be his girlfriend, except that she loved him and had been hoping to make him fall in love with her. And her mom's warning to be careful was too little, too late. What was she going to do? There was no way to protect herself from falling more in love with Ollie.

Tonight, he'd been the perfect date at dinner and games with her parents. Talking about their first date...that had been awkward, but she hoped he'd been sincere when he'd said they'd gone from friends to more. It was what she wanted, but what if that was all he did?

A man didn't ask you to be his fake fiancée if he was hoping for something more solid and committed.

No matter how perfect they seemed here she was going

to have to remember that Ollie hadn't asked her out at first. It was only after he'd kissed her, and that damned sexual attraction had flared between them, that he'd even hinted he might want to date her.

"I wasn't trying to imply anything negative about your family," she said at last. "Just that I'm not sure I'll be as comfortable with them as you were with my family."

"Fair point. I have met your folks a few times before."

"But I've never met yours. Why not? They have come to watch you clown several times," she said.

"I don't know… Actually, I do know," he said sitting down next to her. "I don't always feel like they get the rodeo or my part in it. I guess I just didn't want them to say something in front of you."

She turned so they were facing each other and put her hand on his knee. "Like what?"

He shrugged. "I don't know. My mom would have probably tried to convince you I have other prospects for money and bigged me up to you. That's what she does. It's sort of embarrassing to listen to her go on and on."

Colby shook her head, laughing at the thought of him being embarrassed by his mom. "I can't wait to meet her. What else does she do?"

"Well, set me up with every single woman she meets. She's seriously worried that I'm going to get permanently damaged at the rodeo before I come to my senses. She's not a fan of what I do."

"I get that," she said. "It's dangerous, which I suspect is partially why you do it."

He leaned back and put his legs up on the hassock in front of the couch. "Sort of. But also I like the idea of being the hero. You know? I like distracting the bull until the rider is safely out of the rink. I get some good energy from the crowd."

She could see that. She didn't see him as just a thrill seeker. If he had been, he would have been a bull rider. "So how does someone with your upbringing become a rodeo clown?"

"I don't know if that's something I want to share, Colby-girl, unless you're offering me something intimate."

Intimate.

Just the sound of that word on his lips made heat pulse through her.

"What'd you have in mind?"

"I'll tell you about my path and you tell me something true that you've never shared with anyone else," he said.

"That hardly seems like a good bargain. Surely you becoming a rodeo clown isn't that private."

"It is," he said. "Involves a lot of childhood trauma."

She almost believed him. For a second she was almost sucked in to his aw-shucks kind of talking. But then she saw the glint in his eyes and knew he was playing with her. And after a night of dinner with her folks, playing cards and just feeling like she'd been on edge she needed it. She wanted to laugh and tease and feel young and in love instead of worried and scared.

"Really? Trauma. Like did you have to take the used domestic car to school instead of getting a brand-new luxury foreign one?"

He nodded solemnly at her. "And I didn't get to have the chauffeur drive me."

She laughed out loud at that. "Poor thing. But I'm not buying it. I think your parents might wish you did something else but they never stopped you from going after what you wanted."

"True. But I think they knew that they couldn't stop me once I decided what I wanted."

He turned to face her, leaning in to close the gap between them. "No one can."

Chapter Eight

STOP HIM FROM going after something he wanted.

"Do you want me?" she asked. This was it. She'd been trying to make this into something sensible or make it a game but it wasn't. She wanted him. Sitting in the upstairs game room of her childhood home just drove it home. This was the place where she'd always been herself. No walls or pretending in the Tucker household and now Ollie Rossi was sitting next to her on the overstuffed leather couch and she knew deep in her soul that she wanted him to hold her close.

She didn't need it to be love or for him to lie to her, she just wanted...well Ollie.

"You know I do," he said, pushing himself to his feet and turning away from her. Rubbing his hand over the top of his head as he did. "But we are in your parents' house."

She had to smile at that. Of all the objections she'd expected to hear from him that wasn't one. "So. We're not kids."

"Precisely. I want to be able to make love to you like we deserve. Not a rushed coupling here in the game room. I want it to be special...like you are to me."

Special.

Did that mean love?

Stop it, she warned herself. She wasn't going there. Not anymore. Not tonight. "I like the sound of that."

"Good. As I said I booked us a nice suite at Harwood House in Whiskey River for the entire weekend. It might be nice for us to have the beginning of this next phase of our relationship start there."

She swallowed and tried not to get too excited. "I'd like that. I don't want this to feel rushed or anything."

"Me either," he admitted. "Now I can't sit next to you without wanting to jump your bones so maybe I should head to bed."

"Nah, I'll make sure you keep your hands to yourself. Stay and talk to me," she said.

"What about?"

"Tell me about your family. You said they might be famous, but they are real people." She was curious about them. Wanted to know how she was going to act around them. She didn't want to mess this up because his family didn't like her.

"I'll sit over here," he said, settling into one of the big recliners that was across from the sofa. "Who do you want to know about first?"

"You pick. Who are you closest to?" she asked.

"Hmm. That's a tough one. I'd have to say Angelica. Jock and Nico are closer in age so they have a tight bond. She's...well nothing like that video made her seem. She's very serious about her boutiques and only wants the best for her clients so she has a very demanding attitude toward how they are run. She's sort of used to getting her own way."

"Must be nice," Colby said. To be honest what Ollie was saying completely meshed with her opinion after she'd seen the video. Angelica seemed very demanding and like a type-A personality.

In the video Angelica was sort of going off on a rant. The way it was edited made it seem as if she were berating her staff and talking down about her clients in a negative way.

"Yeah, right."

"Ha. As if you don't get what you want," she teased him.

"I mean I do, but I think I go about it in a nicer way," he said.

He did. Ollie had an easygoing attitude that many people responded to. He didn't have to ask for things to be done his way—most of the time everyone just did it his way.

"Doesn't mean you're not used to getting your own way."

"True. You're not exactly a pushover."

She shook her head. "Didn't say I was. I know that I like things my way."

"You certainly do. But there's nothing wrong with that."

"So who's next?"

"Well I guess Nico," Ollie said. "He and I have gotten closer over the last year or so in the lead-up to Jock's wedding. My mom was over the top trying to matchmake so we've been each other's wingmen. A lot. He's funny, driven, and really good at seeing what makes a person special."

"Special?" she asked, not exactly sure she knew what he meant by that.

"Yeah, like when he meets you, if you said to him you wanted to make money from your life, he'd ask you some questions, and then he'd find the way to show you how to profit from just being you. I don't know how he does it. He just sees what you have that's unique."

She nodded and realized that each of the siblings he'd discussed so far had qualities that Ollie did. He was more like them than she suspected he realized.

"Did he do that for you?" she asked.

He looked away and then nodded as he leaned forward, putting his elbows on his knees. "Yeah. I've been doing some art and he created an online gallery and sells my canvases and some prints of them."

Wait, what? "Why didn't you ever mention it to me?"

"It's sort of private."

"So why tell me now?"

"Things are changing between us, Colby-girl, I don't want to have any secrets from you. No one else knows about it except me and Nico. It's an anonymous site," he said.

Emotions flooded her. A feeling of excitement that he shared it with her, happiness that he acknowledged the changes between them, fear when he said he didn't want any secrets because she had that one big one.

"Thank you for sharing it with me."

He nodded. "Jock's just determined to prove to everyone that he can do whatever they said he couldn't. His former fiancée said he would never be successful at running a restaurant so he's a famous chef with a successful restaurant now. That's his thing."

"That's your thing. A rodeo clown while your parents pressured you to get a degree which you probably don't need...I guess you like to keep things more private."

"I do," he admitted. "Which is going to work in our favor when we get to Whiskey River. Don't feel you have to answer anything any of my family ask you about us."

"Well at least we have the first date down now," she said.

"Yeah we do. I do think of that as our first date; do you?"

OLLIE WAS NO longer sure where this was headed with Colby. Long-term wasn't his thing—he knew that in his core. Just like art, rodeoing, college. He just evolved with each new thing and then moved on; always needed something or someone new. That had to be what this was.

Their first date hadn't been his normal kind of first, but everything had changed on that ride. They hadn't been simply friends after it. And Ollie had always been a man to mark those kinds of changes.

"Yes, I guess I do," she said. "Will your parents ask about it?"

"My dad won't, but my mom and Angelica will. I meant what I said—feel free to tell them to mind their own business." He knew how overwhelming his family could be. They'd driven more than one of the women he'd brought home during high school and college years away. They could be intense at times. There were just so many of them when you counted his cousins. And his family was loud. They always had been.

Tonight with Colby and his parents had been fun and the best part was he hadn't had to yell to be heard over the noise.

"I'm sure I won't have to do that," she said.

"You probably won't. Good luck to any person who wants to get something out of you."

She tipped her head to the side. "So you think I'm secretive?"

"I do," he admitted. "Deny it if you want to but from looking around this house I can see a lot more about you than you've ever revealed to me."

She arched one of her eyebrows at him as she drew her long legs up and wrapped her arms around them, resting her chin on her knees. "Like what?"

"You were a beauty queen."

"I was in the court, not the queen," she said.

As if that made a difference but he didn't know what it was. He'd seen that portrait of her and the one of her sister in the formal living room when they'd walked by it. Colby had taken his breath away. He was used to seeing her as his cowgirl but that woman had been glamorous and sophisticated. The kind of beauty who made men want to make promises they knew they couldn't keep.

Well not men, but himself. He hadn't been expecting that.

"I'm not sure I know the difference."

"Just that I was a runner-up."

"You must have hated that," he said.

"You'd think, but since Mama had made me do it, I wasn't that fussed. I mean if I hadn't even made the court then I would have been," she said. She laughed and shook her head. "I hate it but I'm vain enough to want to have been queen."

But she wasn't vain at all. "If you had really wanted it, you would have gotten it."

She narrowed her eyes. "What are you saying about me, Rossi? That I don't like to lose?"

"Do I really need to say it? I mean everyone who has ever seen you ride knows that." Which was why the beauty queen thing had thrown him. When she was on her horse and riding, it was as if she and the animal were one. She moved with grace and agility. That athleticism almost made him not notice her beauty. Almost.

"Nah, just teasing. I do hate to lose. Was that all you noticed?"

He shook his head.

She tipped her head to the side, clearly waiting for him to go on but he wasn't going to tell her everything he'd learned. He was still processing it. Something about seeing Colby here made him realize that he'd created an image of her that might have nothing to do with the woman she actually was.

Which made him question again why she'd said yes to him when he'd asked her to be his temporary girl.

He refused to ask her again. He was afraid of what she would say. Not because he had a clue what had motivated her but more the opposite. He'd thought they were good friends, but he was coming to realize he might not have been to her. He hadn't really ever looked at her before this.

"Why are you suddenly so quiet?" she asked.

"I don't know how to put the other things into words," he said at last. That was at least partially the truth. "Did you notice anything different about me?"

"Just that you have very good manners and that you like to flirt with everyone," she said.

"It's called being charming," he said, but flushed.

"Is there anything else I should know before we go to Whiskey River tomorrow?" she asked. "I've never been to the town, but everyone has heard of the Kelly family."

"Who are they?"

"Stop it. You have to know who they are," she said.

"Just joshing I do. Nick is a Kelly but didn't know until old Boots died. Not sure if you heard about that bit," he said.

They talked about the town and he caught her up on everything he knew and then he noticed she was starting to get tired. Her eyes kept closing and he knew he should let her go to bed. But he never had this kind of time with her. At the rodeo they were both early to bed so they could be ready for the next day.

She rested her head on her bent knees and looked over at him with those sleepy eyes and he felt a big ol' bolt of emotion that he didn't want and wasn't going to acknowledge.

"Come on, Colby-girl. I'll walk you to your bedroom," he said.

No more sitting across from him and letting temptation make him feel things that he knew he didn't want.

COLBY HADN'T REALIZED how much she'd loved listening to Ollie's voice until tonight. She knew if she walked down the hall to her bedroom with him...well he wouldn't be leaving until morning.

And was that a bad thing? She was too tired to be sensible, so she looked up at him and he watched her in a way she'd never noticed him looking at her before. She could see in his eyes that he didn't want them to go to separate rooms either. She stood up and laced her fingers in his.

He groaned.

She smiled.

He shook his head. "I can't resist you."

"I know."

She'd noticed it when he'd almost kissed her last night by her trailer. She wondered if she should make this easier on him but she couldn't. She'd been wanting him forever and this felt like a road she'd been on for too long and she'd finally arrived at her destination.

It wasn't her fault that he'd just discovered this.

She put her hand on his jaw. She loved that she had the freedom to touch him. Liked the feel of his stubble against her palm and how his pupils dilated slightly at her touch. His hand was on her waist and he pulled her slightly toward him. She leaned into that until her breasts were cushioned against his chest.

She tipped her head back, their eyes met as his finger drew small circles against her waist, which made her heartbeat race but her blood feel as if it were heavy, flowing through her body and awakening all of her senses. She heard the Regulator clock in her parents' foyer chime midnight.

"It's tomorrow."

He grinned at her then, looking young and boyish. "It is. Are you sure you want this? I don't want you to ever have any regrets where I'm concerned."

She already had a million of them. Like why had she waited so long to take this chance to be with him? But she knew the answer. She'd never have made a move because she was afraid to be hurt again. Afraid to trust herself and her heart to any man. But she'd already given her heart to him.

"No regrets."

She said the words out loud because they were as much for herself as they were for Ollie. She needed to hear them so that this moment would feel more real. So she'd know she wasn't just imagining it.

"Me either. Uh, one question…are you on the pill?" he asked. "I have some condoms in my bathroom bag."

"Of course you do, rodeo stud."

"Does that bother you?" he asked.

"Yes," she said, but hadn't meant to. "Sorry. It's not my business."

"It wasn't but it is now. You know all my past escapades… What about you? You mentioned a guy—"

"I don't want to talk about that," she said quickly. She pulled back realizing that she was screwing this up even when she'd been trying not to. Was it any surprise she hadn't ever made a move toward him? She just never had the right kind of chill to handle acting casual around a man she liked.

"Yeah, it's awkward isn't it? So I'm thinking I broke the mood, but so I don't have to do it again, are you on the pill?"

"No, I'm not."

"Okay. I'll take care of it when the time is right," he said. "I'm sorry I've been a bit of a man slut."

"No you're not sorry and I never thought of you as a

man slut," she said not wanting him to believe something that wasn't true. "You really are a natural flirt. Everyone likes you and I'd be surprised if you didn't have women falling at your feet."

"But not you," he said. "You always looked straight through my alleged charm and made me feel—"

He broke off.

What? "What did I make you feel?" Colby asked, curious.

"Never you mind, Colby-girl. My mama always says nothing good happens after midnight and I think I finally understand why."

Colby suspected she did too. The truth was just easier after midnight, as if the barriers of daytime and real life were lowered. As if consequences didn't really exist in this place.

"Me too. Good night, Ollie," she said, turning and walking toward her bedroom before she did something even dumber than mentioning the reason why he had condoms.

"Good night, Colby."

He let her leave, probably for the same reason. She washed up in her private bathroom and then lay on her bed staring at the ceiling, wondering if she was ever going to figure out how to do this with Ollie.

Because this was the one place where she was her most confident...except for on the back of a horse. How did that make sense? But it was true. She'd never been the beauty in the portrait downstairs.

She'd always been a cowgirl. Sure, her mama had made sure she knew how to pretty up and look good but inside she always felt her best when she was in her jeans, on the back of her horse.

And until she'd had to face the truth of Ollie tonight she'd thought he was too. But there was a lot more to the man than the parts she saw each rodeo season. Those few months when she'd fallen for him, never knowing that he was so much more than she'd thought she knew.

She rolled to her side and looked at the clock. Only twenty minutes had passed. This was going to be a long night. And she had a feeling the weekend might be long too. She wasn't sure how she was going to handle his family or the special hotel weekend he'd planned.

She was both excited and scared. She wanted Ollie and she needed this weekend to be more than special. She needed it to be the kind of first she'd forgotten that she wanted.

Chapter Nine

WHISKEY RIVER WAS a smallish town in the Texas Hill Country. It had the kind of charm that Georgetown and neighboring Last Stand did. But she noticed as they drove toward the outskirts of town and the Rancho Del Rey—the family homestead of the Rossis—that Ollie got more tense. Honestly, he got less like the man she knew and more of a stranger.

Of course the morning had been awkward at first—mainly on her side. She hadn't known what to say or how to act. She was tired from a restless night and once they got on the road, Ollie had tuned in to a local country music station, discouraging conversation. She had thought it was the way they'd parted the night before but now she was beginning to think it might be his family. She knew it was for her because she'd given in to her own fear.

"I'm sure your family is going to be happy to see you," she said. Not sure what was making him tense.

"I know they are," he said, cursing under his breath and then smiling over at her. "Sorry I've been a moody SOB this morning."

He offered no explanation as to why he had been. "That's all right. I've been rereading *Wuthering Heights* so you put me in a mind of Heathcliff."

"That's not exactly reassuring," he said.

She just winked at him. "Have you ever heard that song by Kate Bush?"

"About what?"

"*Wuthering Heights*. You have to hear it. Let me find it," she said. There was no way that Ollie would be moody after listening to that song. It was a performance art sort of song with a high-pitched chanteuse singing the basic plot of *Wuthering Heights*. She and her sister had discovered it when they'd been going through a classics phase. The song was so odd but at the same time catchy.

"Here it is," she said, finding it on her smartphone app and then connecting wirelessly to Ollie's truck's radio. The song started with sort of chimes and a piano and then that high-pitched singing.

Ollie gave a bark of laughter. "Definitely haven't heard this before."

He was listening to the words and she started singing along with Kate Bush but in a lower octave, which made him smile. Still not sure what was bothering him but happy that her silly singing had cheered him up, she waited until the song was over. "I used this instead of reading the book, aced the test."

"Liar."

She was. "Yeah, I guess I am. I'm not a very good liar."

He signaled and pulled the truck off to the side of the road. Putting the truck in park, he turned to face her. "I'm sorry I'm making you lie. I realized this morning as your parents were hugging us both before we left that I've put us both in the worst position. I'm not saying that there was any way you'd be here without me asking you to lie. But I wish I hadn't had to do that."

"Me too," she admitted. More than he'd ever know. Or maybe one day she'd tell him the truth. Everything was depending on this weekend. Once she they slept together, she knew everything would be different.

"That's what I was apologizing for."

"So why are you tense?"

"I'm not tense. Sorry, my family sometimes makes me feel like my skin is too small for my body," he said.

"I get that. But you're not alone this time. You've got me by your side," she said.

"I do. I just don't want to hurt you," he said.

She sort of had been feeling the same way about him, though wasn't truly sure whether to believe what he said to her, but last night in her parents' game room she'd realized that he had barriers same as she did. His were just different. She hadn't been able to really figure out what it was about him and his family that was getting to him.

Maybe meeting his folks would make that obvious.

"I'd rather not be hurt either," she admitted.

"Do you want to stop this now?" he asked. "I would make sure they knew it was all me."

Was he kidding? After she'd told her parents they were sort of dating? He had to be testing her, which ticked her off. So she decided turnabout was fair play.

"Fine. Drop me off in town. I'll see you back at the rodeo," she said. She had a tough time with new people and going to a charity gala with a man who had pretended she was his fiancée and then changed his mind wasn't what she had in mind. "This isn't like you."

"What?"

"Changing your mind. Is it me or yourself you doubt? It has to be me. Do you think I can't pull this off?" she asked. "Or is it that I'm not enough for you and your overachiever family? I don't have a secret degree, you know."

"Hell. I didn't mean that. I just realized that this could backfire on us the closer I got to home. You ever have that? Where an idea seems good until you know your parents are going to hear it?"

"Yes. But then you pulled up behind me and my dad came around the side of the house and things worked out," she said.

"It's not you," he said, reaching over to touch the side of her face and then he leaned even further over and kissed her. There was so much intensity in the kiss, she felt it all the way to her core. "I want to do this together. I like having you by my side."

He was trying to tell her something that words wouldn't convey. She kissed him back, put her hands on his shoulders and held him to her so he wouldn't leave just yet. But he wasn't going anywhere. He took his time kissing her and when he lifted his head and their eyes met, she knew that whatever he'd been debating about had been resolved. "We got this."

"Yeah, we do," she agreed, but she was no longer sure of that.

OLLIE HAD SPENT the previous night trying to make sure that he didn't fuck this up and do something stupid. He also needed to give her an out. He wasn't proud of himself for testing her the way he had but he'd rather she break down when they were alone, than in front of his mom who had always had a pretty good bullshit detector.

Thing was that Colby was honest. She wasn't lying about being attracted to him—that kiss had confirmed it and he knew that if he were a smarter man, he would have focused on that instead of giving himself a mental high five that his plan was still intact. He should be more concerned about the real-life consequences of this but instead he just wanted…peace.

That's what he wanted. He was almost always moving and trying to figure out what made him stand out in his family and nothing did. He was just the third son. That was it.

When they pulled up at his parents' large ranch house that had been redone and remodeled just last year, she caught her breath. The house was impressive—all stone and masonry in the front that had been locally sourced. He parked behind Nico's red sports car and got out to go around and open Colby's door but she was already out and standing there.

She stood taller than he'd seen her before, and he realized that his "test" hadn't helped her nerves. In fact he'd probably made it worse. "I'm an ass."

"No you're not. But why?"

"I should have been helping you relax before we got here," he said.

"You definitely should have but to be fair nothing could have prepared me for this mansion or the luxury cars in the drive," she said.

"You know my family has money," he responded. His family was always another reason why he didn't really bring any women home. The wealth brought out a different side to his dates at times.

He waited to see how Colby reacted.

"I saw someone in the window watching us. They are probably wondering what's going on with us," she said. "We should go in."

He took her hand in his and started walking to the front door. This weekend was going to be a crucible and at the end of it he'd know…well who the fuck was he kidding? He had no clue what it was going to be. He just hoped when it was over that Colby would still be by his side.

The door opened as they approached and his mom was standing there. "Hey, Ollie. Sorry if you saw me looking out the window. I wasn't sure if I heard your truck or not."

"We didn't notice," he said, going over to kiss her cheek and give her a hug. "Mama, this is Colby. Colby, this is my mother, Rosa—"

"Call me Mama Rosa—everyone does," she said, coming over to give Colby a hug. "Welcome to our home. Get y'all's bags, Ollie."

She looped her arm through Colby's and started walking into the house. He could hear his mother asking about the drive. Ollie stood there, wondering why his mom thought they were staying here when he'd told her they were staying at Harwood House.

He just took his time, following them onto the patio where there were drinks and snacks waiting along with his sister Angelica, his dad and his brother Jock.

Hell.

He should have expected this after the Zoom call. But still.

His mom made the introductions as Ollie poured them both a glass of iced tea and sat down next to his brother.

"How was the drive?"

"Good. We were just coming from her folks's in

Georgetown, so not really a long one."

"That's good. Met the parents. How'd that go?"

"Good. They are really nice. I've met them before at the rodeo. They come and watch Colby ride a couple of times during the season."

"Why didn't we meet her when Nico and I came to visit you?" he asked.

"Because I don't like you in my business," Ollie said. He had had time to think about the fact that while his parents didn't come to the rodeo that often, his brothers came whenever he was close to one of them.

"Uh-huh."

"What's that mean?"

"Nothing," Jock said. "Delilah is coming over after she sets up for dinner."

"That's good. Why aren't you over in Last Stand at Laissez Faire?" he asked. His brother had opened a restaurant almost two years ago, but he only ran the kitchens when he was in town. For about six months a year he was in New York filming his television cooking show.

"I wanted to be here when you arrived," Jock said.

"Why?"

"Hadn't seen you in a bit and you haven't brought a woman home before," Jock said.

"He hasn't?" Colby said, coming over and sitting on his knee. He put his arms around her waist and kissed her.

"Nope."

"Well then I guess I'm special," Colby said.

"I can tell you are," Jock said.

Ollie realized that if anyone was going to blow this it was him. He was the one who was awkward with his family. Colby was at ease. The fiancée meeting the family for the first time but clearly with the man she loved.

Loved.

He felt that all the way to his soul. Did he want her to love him?

He wasn't sure he wanted to love her. Or could. He'd never loved anyone before but holding her on his lap while they talked to his brother, he realized that he definitely didn't want to let her go at the end of June. As soon as they were alone, he needed to make her his, tie her to him any way he could. For the first time in his dating life he'd found a woman he wanted to keep and he had no idea how he was going to do that.

COLBY REALIZED THAT the hardest part in convincing Ollie's family that they were a couple was Ollie. She hadn't ever really seen her charming rodeo clown act this way around anyone else. But he had been defensive with his brother until she'd come and sat down with them. His sister kept watching him and she knew that he wasn't being himself.

When his parents left the table Angelica came over to sit next to them. "What's up with you, Ollie?"

"Nothing."

"You're acting tense and Mom and Dad will eventually notice or Mom will when she stops smiling at the fact that you have a fiancée," Angelica said.

"It's just that I don't want you guys to scare Colby off," he said. "I finally got a woman I really like and don't want the family to mess it up."

She liked the way he played it. To be honest that sentiment felt like the truth to her. "They can't scare me off. I'm tougher than that."

"I know you are," he said, turning his face and smiling up at her and for the first time she wasn't sure if he was faking or not. There was an adoring look in his eyes that she'd never seen before. A part of her was sure it was for his siblings but that silly part of her that had said yes to this farce wanted to believe it.

Saw it for the infatuation she'd been craving for much too long. She turned away from him and scooted off his lap to sit next to his sister. Ollie had a lot more going on than she'd realized.

"So you two met at the rodeo?" Angelica said.

"Yes. We've been friends for years but recently...well, things started to change," Colby said.

"You mean my brother finally wised up," Angelica said.

"Something like that. Jock, you're married, right?"

"Yes. My wife is the chef-owner of the Dragonfly in Last Stand," he said. It was sort of out-of-body to be talking to

Jock like he was a regular guy. Which he totally was.

"My mom loves your show," Colby said. "She is hoping you'll come out with a cookbook."

"Tell your mom I said thanks for watching. My team wants me to do one too, but that's not my thing," he said. "I find I do better when I stay in my wheelhouse."

There was something almost normal about him. In fact, he was Ollie's brother not a celebrity chef. This was her chance to get to know about Ollie. "What was he like as a kid?"

"Colby—"

Jock laughed and shook his head. "Not sure I want to go there. My wife has been trying to get the dirt on me from these two."

"Not trying," Angelica said. "I'll hook you up with the info you need later."

Ollie just groaned but good-heartedly and things sort of shifted into place. She felt she'd garnered a little insight into what he was doing here with his family. What he needed from her. He had pretty much told her how he'd felt like he never fit in and now she got it. She saw what he meant by that.

With her, he had something that was an equalizer. No one was going to ask him when he was leaving the rodeo while she was here. No one was going to press him for whatever it was that he didn't want to share. Well, except her. She needed to know what it was he wanted to avoid.

"Are y'all staying here?"

"No. I booked us a room at the Harwood," Ollie said.

"Olivier, you are breaking my heart," his mom said. "Why can't you stay here?"

"Mama, we live in trailers all the time and sort of rough it. I thought it would be a nice treat for Colby to have room service, a warm bath in a big tub...you know, spoil my girl for the weekend."

She was on board until the last part. He was putting it on a little thick and now that she wasn't sure if he was playing her as well as his family she wasn't as charmed by him. She knew she'd been taking a gamble when she'd agreed to this. She'd made herself at least acknowledge the fact that he might not fall for her. But this...she hadn't counted on falling harder for Ollie. Or the fact that he might not fall for her. She'd thought he'd fall in love with her or she'd fall out of love, not that she'd become even more deeply entrenched in her own emotions while he remained unchanged.

Hadn't seen a scenario where he'd use her...suddenly she wondered if he'd somehow figured out how she felt about him. Was this his way of ticking two things off the list?

"That does sound nice. Reminds me of when your dad and I were courting and he flew me to Rome for dinner."

"Papa is good at romantic gestures," Ollie said.

"Yeah, he's my go-to man when I need to get out of the doghouse," Jock said.

"Are you in there a lot?" she asked, but his comments made her realize that perhaps she was feeling a little vulnerable here. Because Ollie might just be doing something his family expected from him.

"More often than I want to be. But Delilah's..."

"Yes?" Angelica said.

"The best wife a man could have," Jock admitted.

"Seems like all of my boys have found the best women for them," Mama Rosa said. "I think you're going to fit in here very well, Colby. Welcome to our family."

She smiled over at the older woman and felt a little scuzzy for the first time since she'd agreed to deceive his family. "Thank you, Mama Rosa. I'm looking forward to being a part of it."

"Speaking of that...have you set a date?"

"Not yet. We don't want to until after Nico and Cressida are married. The spotlight is on them," Ollie said. He reached over to take Colby's hand in his and kissed the back of her knuckles before he looked over at her and their eyes met. "But we don't plan to wait too long."

Chapter Ten

BOOTS & BANGLES was the social event of the spring in Whiskey River and everyone who was anyone attended. Ollie was waiting at the foot of the stairs at the Harwood House hotel for Colby who'd asked him to give her some privacy while she got ready for the evening.

"Ollie, dude, good to see you."

He turned to see Gage Powell a former bull rider who'd married a few years back and had stopped riding full-time.

"Gage, good to see you. What are you doing in Whiskey River?" he asked, after they exchanged a bro hug.

"I'm here for Boots & Bangles. Got hooked up with a pair of Kelly Boots from Nick. What are you doing here?"

"Same. My folks moved to Whiskey River about a year and a half ago and my entire family is attending."

"Yeah? Can't wait to meet the rest of your clan," Gage said.

"Do you live here now?"

"Sort of part-time. Nick and I have been working on a stud program for bulls. I want to hear more about how our bulls did last weekend. Nick said they were pretty good,"

Gage said.

"Yeah, they were. I was impressed. How did I not know this about you? I was here at Christmas."

Gage rubbed the back of his neck and shook his head. "We headed to the wife's family for the holidays and then stopped by my folks in Oklahoma."

Gage looked over Ollie's shoulder and let out a wolf whistle. "Damn, woman, you just keep getting hotter each time I see you."

"You have never been a sweet-talker, Gage Powell, but thanks for the compliment."

Ollie turned to see Sierra Montez Powell standing there. She was pretty and everything but in his mind he knew that Colby was prettier. Gage's wife was the daughter of the heritage jeans company who often sponsored events at the bigger rodeos. He'd met her a time or two in the past.

"Ollie? I hardly recognize you all duded up," she said. "You here for the gala?"

"I am. Just waiting on my woman."

"If you want to keep her, maybe don't let her hear you calling her that," she said with a wink.

"I'm a bit smarter than I must look," he said with a wink in return.

"Glad to hear that," Gage said. "We'll see you at the gala."

He waved goodbye to the couple. It was nice to see them still happy together. He was coming to realize there was a lot more in Whiskey River to make it home than he'd previously realized. He'd been trying to keep his distance because of old hurts from his family but he was seeing so many connections and of course with Colby by his side today, he was seeing everything a bit differently.

It had almost backfired more than once. His family for some reason brought out the worst in him. He could be his regular self when he was at the rodeo because it was so foreign to the Rossi world. But once he was back with them…all bets were off.

He heard the elevator bell ping and looked up as the doors opened and Colby walked out of the car. She had her long brown hair curled and piled up on her head with a tendril hanging down on the left side of her face. She had on makeup and looked more beautiful than she had in the portrait in her parents' home.

The dress she wore was some kind of lacy bodice that hugged her torso before it flared out in a floor-length gown. Their eyes met and he realized that all the guessing and playing he'd been doing were at an end. He couldn't try to pretend there was anything fake about why he was with this woman.

He wanted her. Wanted her in his bed and under his body. Wanted her next to him on the drive, talking and teasing. Wanted her by his side on horseback as they rode through fields.

She hesitated at the top step and he just continued to

stare at her before his manners kicked in and went up the few steps to offer her his arm. She slipped her hand into the crook of his arm.

"You are gorgeous. I mean I thought you were beautiful as the beauty queen but this…you take my breath away."

She flushed and tucked her chin down before smiling sort of shyly at him. "Thanks. I'm always sure that I won't remember how to pretty up."

"You don't have to worry about that," he said.

They started walking down the stairs, but she stopped. "You look nice in your tux."

"Thank you."

"I kind of feel like we are both playing a part tonight. I mean this isn't how I normally see us."

He wondered what she meant by that. Hoped that maybe she hadn't felt like they'd been playing parts over the last few days. He had been but from this moment forward he wouldn't anymore.

Couldn't really.

Something had changed inside of him when he'd seen her tonight and that wasn't going to go back to the way things had been.

He might want to say that he was the odd Rossi, the one who didn't fit in, but he knew that was a lie.

He wanted to make this night as romantic for her as he could and he refused to examine why that was. He'd never been good at doing the expected thing. Never good at fitting in and staying where he was supposed to.

And a part of him knew that even if tonight he thought that was what he wanted, he'd always be hungry and restless, always be moving to the next thing. Because that was what he had always done.

He might not like that about himself, but he'd never shied away from telling himself the truth. They took the limo he'd booked to the Boots & Bangles event. The entire time Colby talked about how excited she was to have this night out and to dance with him.

And all he could think of was how excited he was to have her by his side. For this night.

COLBY WAS A bit surprised that the entire Rossi family were all very sociable, even Ollie who wasn't acting odd around her anymore. She still wasn't sure what had been on his mind earlier when they'd been at his family's home, but he was drinking beer and acting a lot more like the guy she knew. Despite the fact that they were both dressed to the nines she felt more comfortable now than she had earlier.

They had dinner and the auction went quickly and soon the deejay was playing party hits from all the decades and inviting them onto the dance floor. Colby loved to dance but hadn't in a long time. There just wasn't occasion to go to dances in her line of work.

But Ollie and his siblings and their dates all hit the dance floor and she found herself in a group with them.

"I'm sorry I didn't get to meet you earlier," Delilah Corbyn Rossi said. Jock's wife was blond, petite and incredibly chatty.

"Me too. My mom and some of her friends had lunch at the Dragonfly last fall and haven't stopped talking about it," Colby said.

"Why thank you. Jock already told me she's a fan of his show. I'm not sure his ego can take many more compliments," Delilah said.

"Should I not have mentioned it?"

"No way. My mom and meemaw fawn over him all the time," she admitted. "He's a damned good chef. So you and Ollie…"

"Me and Ollie what?"

"How'd you two go from being friends to lovers?" Delilah asked. "My sister did that with her husband. I have never met a guy and thought yeah, let's be friends and then realized later he was hot."

Colby laughed. She liked Delilah. "I know it's crazy. Let me say I knew he was hot when we met but friends seemed the smarter choice. Ollie's a bit of a player."

"Heard he's more than a bit," Delilah said. "Jock likes to talk when he's had too much to drink—actually all the Rossis do. I heard all kinds of gossip back at Christmas."

"Good to know," she said.

"So you're engaged?" Delilah asked.

"Yes...why don't we seem engaged?" Colby realized that made it sound suspicious.

"You do. Did you set a date?"

"Not yet," she said. "We are waiting until after Nico's wedding. But we have been working on a website that we are going to share with family and friends soon."

"You have been? My mom totally wanted me to do that but it's just not me. She set one up and I made her take it down. Jock's fans were all finding it..."

"Is it hard being married to someone famous?" Colby asked. The more she got to know the Rossi family the more she realized how much she actually liked them. Not the images of who they had been before but the real people.

"Sometimes. Most of the time it isn't because I'm here cooking and doing my thing and in Last Stand everyone treats Jock like he's just another dude. But when he's filming on location it's different."

"Do you go with him?"

"Not often. I really like staying close to home and being in my restaurant. I guess you and Ollie both like being on the road?"

"I think so. We're both sort of wanderers."

"I can see that," she said.

Jock and Ollie both came over to them. "What are you two discussing?" Jock asked his wife as he pulled her into his arms.

"Which of you is the most arrogant," Delilah said.

"I hope you said it was me," Jock retorted.

"I tried."

"But Ollie is pretty hard to knock off the top spot," Colby said. "He's used to strutting around the ring and listening to applause after he saves a rider from 1900 pounds of raging bull."

"And that makes me arrogant? I do save the day a lot. I guess I'm sort of a hero," Ollie said.

He was to her, she thought. She wrinkled her nose at him and nodded. "You are. But you also have a big head about it. I'm surprised you can get your cowboy hat to ever stay on."

That made Jock laugh. The music changed to "We Are Family" and Delilah grabbed her arm. "Dance time!"

She followed Delilah with Ollie behind her holding her hand. He tugged her off-balance and into his arms.

"Are you having fun?"

"I am. Are you?"

"Yes. You seem to get along very well with my family," he said, as they moved to the music and danced closer to each other.

"I do. They are a lot like you," she said.

He gave her a quizzical look but then Angelica danced between them, which stopped them from talking.

"You two are so cute. I love it," Angelica said. "I never thought Ollie would let another woman into his heart after Mia. I'm so glad he found you."

Angelica hugged her and the smell of champagne was strong on her breath. She hugged the other women back, wondering who Mia was and whether she was the reason for the fake engagement.

Ollie pulled Angelica back and led her off the dance floor and Colby followed, going to the bar to get some water for his sister.

When she got back and handed Angelica the water, she took a deep swallow as Colby turned to Ollie.

"What did my sister say to you?"

"Why?"

"Your face turned white," he said.

"She mentioned a woman called Mia and said that she was glad you let me into your heart."

"Oh."

"Yeah, oh. We can talk about that later."

Ollie didn't say anything else as his parents arrived and bundled Angelica out of the party. She knew that Angelica had gotten word that afternoon that she was being sued, which explained the heavy drinking. But the stuff about Ollie... She turned to face him and as their eyes met, she realized that she didn't really know him at all.

FUCK. DOUBLE FUCK. This was why he avoided his family. He had never intended for Colby to know anything about Mia. Now there was no way he could avoid talking about her.

She was waiting for him to say something, but he had no idea where to start and frankly didn't want to talk about it.

"I'm going to get a drink. Want one?"

"Yes. But I want answers too," she said.

"Not now. I'm not doing this here," he said.

"Doing what exactly?" she asked. She didn't know what exactly he hadn't told her, and it was clear to Ollie that she wasn't sure what was in this Pandora's box that Angelica had opened.

"Talking about her or the past," he said maneuvering his way through the crowd. He wished he was a little drunk or totally drunk. Then he would have no problem either ignoring the fact that she wanted answers from him, or he would just blurt it all out.

But he wasn't drunk.

Not yet.

He was in line for the cash bar and she was right behind him. He could smell her perfume and feel the heat from her body.

And, well, fuck.

He wanted to just enjoy this evening with this woman instead of having to wrestle with ghosts from his past. Which shouldn't have been stirring at all. He'd lain them to rest a long time ago.

But damned Angelica always thought Mia was the reason he was still single. And that Mia was the reason he'd left

Louisiana and never gone back. Mia was the reason why he'd friend-zoned Colby. Hell. That was a truth he hadn't been aware of until that moment.

"Jack and Coke, please. Colby?"

"Spicy marg," she said to the bartender.

Ollie looked over at her and wondered why he had never connected these two women before? Maybe because he hadn't wanted to see the connection? He took his wallet out and paid for the drinks and left a generous tip.

Colby linked her arm through his and walked with him—not toward their table or the crowded dance floor but to an empty table at the edge of the party. She raised her glass to his and their eyes met.

He clinked his glass against hers and took a long, fortifying sip.

"So…ex?"

"Yes. I really don't want to do this now," he said.

"Fair enough. Let's drink and pretend neither of us has a past," she said.

That sounded too good to be true, but then he reminded himself this was Colby. She'd been his friend and probably his best friend for more than five years. She understood him better than he did himself most of time.

"Deal."

He took another swallow, but he couldn't just sit here. Colby deserved better from him. The fact that she had said neither of them had a past meant she had something too.

Which made sense. They were both ramblers, following the rodeo from town to town for a reason. No one just left home and didn't put down reasons without one.

"So your past—"

"Don't. If you're not talking neither am I."

He nodded, took another sip. "This deejay is pretty good."

She threw her head back and let out one of her deep laughs and he couldn't help smiling. "He is. The food was pretty good too."

He saw what she was doing and why she'd laughed. They were both back in default stranger mode. Not talking about the real things because the one topic that needed discussing he'd taken off the table.

The deejay was talking but Ollie wasn't listening to a word he said. He just watched Colby, seeing the delicate beauty of her face, but he knew that she was strong. Probably stronger than he was. He wasn't sure what was in her past but he knew that it hadn't driven her away from home. Not the way that Mia had driven him.

The fact that no one in his family ever discussed it made it harder for him to be at home.

"You don't have to tell me anything," she said, softly. "We're not really anything to each other."

Her words cut like a rusty a knife because he knew that she was starting to become everything to him. Which was probably why he'd gone about asking her out in this back-ass way. But he was still too good at shutting down and not letting anyone else see how he felt. He had no real idea how to break through and show her what she meant to him.

"We are so much more than either of us have ever realized. I want to show you, but not here. I promise."

"And you always keep your word, don't you?" she asked.

"I do. It's the one thing you can count on me to do."

"I know," she said. "Want to dance and live like we're young? Pretend that the past isn't a weight that is aging us more than either of us wants to admit."

"Hell, yes. Tell me your favorite party song. I'll go and request it."

"'Can't Feel My Face,'" she said.

"Really?"

"Yeah. Why?"

"Thought you'd be more 'Redneck Woman,'" he said.

"Sometimes I am but tonight I think I need The Weeknd."

Once again, she was surprising him. She was strong, tough and that was something he admired in her.

They went and asked the deejay for their song and he warned them he might not get to it, but Nico came over and informed him that they were newly engaged, and he bumped their song to the top of the queue.

As the song came on Colby started to dance along with it. His brothers, Delilah and Cressida joined them and soon they were all dancing and singing together in a group and for a brief moment the music swept everything else away. Nico and Cressida danced pressed together, and he saw Delilah dancing around Jock. When his eyes met Colby's he realized he'd been waiting for another woman since Mia had left. No not just any other woman, which all those one-night stands had proven. He'd been waiting for Colby.

Chapter Eleven

A N EX THAT he didn't want to talk about. She'd done her best to ignore it for the rest of the evening and it had been easy when they'd been dancing, and the music had been loud enough to make it impossible to really think, but now they were in the limo on the way back to the hotel. And Ollie was sitting next to her on the long bench, not really talking but seeming like he was waiting for her to.

And for once she didn't want to. She wanted to go back to when she was in love with a guy that it turned out she hardly knew. At this exact moment she didn't know if she still loved him. It was hard to say when she was looking at a man who was a stranger, still. And she'd had a chance to get to know him better than she'd expected to.

"I suppose—"

"Don't do that, don't pretend that you have to tell me something because I want to know," she said. She might want to be with Ollie but she still respected herself and she wasn't going to allow him to turn this on her.

"You're right, I'm sorry. I saw this night going a different way," he said.

"I did too," she admitted. She sat there for a minute getting all in her head and then realized that there were two ways this could go. His ex was going to be there in the morning for them to discuss or to not talk about. But this night could still be salvaged. She had to just let go of those ideas she had of how perfect a man Ollie was and accept him with his feet of clay.

Maybe she shouldn't have been surprised at how much of a dual life Ollie had been living. He'd admitted that he kept this rodeo life separate from his...well, real life for lack of a better word. But this felt big. Like something that maybe she should have picked up on sooner.

She should have guessed he was more than a player with all those one-night stands. Maybe he'd been trying to exorcise the ghost of his ex. Had he done it yet?

Was this fake engagement one more attempt?

"I mean I did buy this sexy-ass dress and it's so skintight I can't wear underwear," she said.

That got his attention. He sat up a little straighter but didn't move, just shifted his gaze, his eyes skimming over her body. Down the skintight bodice and then back up to her face.

"I didn't realize that," he said. "Actually how is that possible? You were jumping up and down and dancing and your boobs—never mind. I don't need to know. I guess it's woman magic."

"It is. In fact, I've got a few more woman magic secrets

hidden in here," she said, even though she doubted that stick-on bra cups were magic.

He scooted toward her on the long leather seat, one arm going along the back of the bench, draping over her shoulders, the other lightly falling on her lap. He leaned in, moving his head toward hers. His breath smelled of Jack and Coke and his eyes were serious, but she couldn't read his emotions. Did that matter?

Heck no. She was going to get it on with this man tonight. Tomorrow everything could go to hell, but she'd have this one night. It wasn't perfect but neither had the two of them ever been.

She put her hand on his jaw because this was the only time she felt comfortable touching him. And the façade she'd been working so hard to keep in place since he'd suggested she be his fake fiancée dropped. She let the emotions she was working to balance flow free and for the first time she didn't care if he realized she really liked him.

Stop thinking.

She brushed her lips over his, shifting up a little to get a better position, and then his mouth opened under his and their tongues brushed, so softly and delicately that she shivered. Awareness spread through her like tequila through her veins. She wanted so much more than this sweet kiss, but she tucked this in the back of her heart for much later.

The second time his tongue brushed over hers was anything but tentative. He took control of the kiss as he wrapped his arms around her and he lifted her onto his lap. She felt the ridge of his cock against her hip and knew he was turned on. She was warm and moist in her center and her breasts were full, her nipples aching little points. One of his hands drew down the center of her back. Moving toward her butt, cupping it as he urged her to straddle him. She pulled her mouth from his.

"I need to get my balance," she said. "You know a ride's no good unless I'm in the saddle right."

He threw his head back and laughed. "Colby-girl, damn, I like you."

His face filled with this joy and totally relaxed was something she'd never seen before. She took a moment to commit that to her heart, then lifted the hem of her dress and heard his gasped intake of breath as he noticed that she was indeed not wearing any panties.

She felt his fingers on her thigh and then higher on her hip. She stayed still, letting him caress and explore her. She held her breath and realized that this moment—this moment that wasn't perfect but was so damned real—was one she'd been waiting for longer than she wanted to admit. His fingers were on her center, his fingers moving over her and sending tingles that made her shiver.

He parted her and touched the most delicate part of her body. She closed her eyes, her head falling back as he caressed her, and he trapped her in a sensual web that made everything else disappear.

She felt his arm around her back, twisting her on the seat until she was lying on her back and he was between her legs. His fingers parting her and then his tongue on her, tasting her and driving her higher and higher. She arched her hips toward him, her thighs on either side of his head, his thick hair against her legs. He kept tasting her and driving her higher and higher until she felt his finger thrust up inside of her and she clenched down hard on it, coming in a long gasp, calling his name.

THE LIMO SLOWED down just as Colby came and Ollie savored one last taste of this woman who was coming to mean more to him than he wanted to admit as he sat up. Delicately moving his legs so that his erection was caught uncomfortably in his pants. He pulled the skirt of her dress down her legs as she sat up next to him. The car rolled to a stop and her eyes got wide.

"Damn, Ollie, you have really good timing," she said.

She kept surprising him and maybe he needed to stop expecting her to be like anyone else. Colby was so uniquely her.

"I know."

The driver opened the back door and they both got out of the car. They went into the lobby, which wasn't too busy, but he noticed a few other couples that had been at the gala were staggering back to their rooms. When they got to the elevator, Colby stood in front of him and he felt her hand stroking his cock as they waited for the car.

He caught her wrist and linked their fingers together, leaning down to kiss the long line of her neck, then nipped at the lobe of her ear. "If you do that I'll come in my pants and not in you."

He felt her shiver against him. "Well that'd be a shame."

The car arrived and they got on and had it to themselves and he groaned because he was so tempted to start something in here, but he didn't have a condom on him, and he hadn't been lying when he'd told her he wanted their first time to be unhurried.

She turned toward him, and he groaned again. Colby seemed to be playing by her own rules. He felt her hand on the zipper of his pants and his cock jumped.

"No. I'm not kidding. I want you too much," he said.

"Just checking," she said. The car arrived on their floor and the doors opened. She walked out of the car and down the hallway, slowly, her hips swaying provocatively with each step. She tapped her keycard to unlock their door and turned back, looking at him over her shoulder.

"Hurry up."

His cock got even harder as he walked down that hallway and stepped into their suite. She'd left the light on in the sitting area and it provided an intimate glow. She was standing there leaning back against the wall, waiting for him. He went past her straight into the bathroom and got a condom before things went any further. He tucked it into his pocket and came back in the hall of their room where she was still waiting for him.

He put his hand on the wall behind her head and leaned close until his chest rubbed her breasts and his hips touched hers, his erection nestling in the notch of her thighs. He moved his hips, letting the sweet torture of her body build the excitement inside of him.

She pushed his tuxedo jacket off his arms, and he shrugged out of it, letting it fall to the floor. She undid his bow tie next and tossed it on the floor before going for his buttons. He liked the feel of her fingers on him, undressing him, but he was longing to touch her too. So he skimmed his hand down her side, sure that the zipper had to be nestled in there. He found it and drew it down.

The fabric of her dress gapped away from her body and he slipped his hand inside the back along her smooth skin and the warmth at the small of her back. She arched against him as she ran her hands up his chest to his shoulders and pushed his shirt off.

It caught at his wrists since she hadn't undone his cuffs. She made quick work of that and soon he was shirtless and her hands were roaming over his body. Her fingers lingered on the tattoo over his heart that said *Tin Man*. Tracing over the script.

"Why?"

"So I never forget," he said.

He was afraid she'd ask another question, so he brought his mouth down on hers, shoving his free hand into her hair and pulling out the pins that held it in place until her hair hung down around her shoulders. Her fingers were slowly working on the button of his pants and then the zipper.

She pushed her hand into his underwear and stroked his cock. She smiled as he was kissing her. He thrust against her. Reaching into his pocket and drawing out the condom.

He broke their kiss, stepping back and taking a moment to draw the dress down her body, and she stepped out of it, still wearing a pair of impossibly high heels. He knelt carefully at her feet and undid the straps and she stepped out of them, her hand on his shoulder as he did so.

Then he kissed her thigh and smelled her sex, which made him forget about his careful plans. That he wanted to make this last and take his time with her. Suddenly he just had to be inside of her. Had to claim her and make sure she knew she was his.

He stood and lifted her more in a fireman's carry than anything romantic sweeping her up, and carried her to the bed, dropping her on it and coming down over her, one hand by her head as he brought his mouth down on hers, taking it with the same dominance he knew he was going to take her body. Her thighs parted and rubbed against his hips as she rubbed her moist center down the length of his naked cock and he knew that he wasn't going to last much longer. He fumbled with the condom and Colby took it from him.

"Let me."

She undid the packet and then put it on him. And he stood there shuddering, taking deep breaths until he got himself sort of under control.

COLBY HADN'T EXPECTED to feel this free, this sensual, this alive. But she knew that was due to years of hiding how she really felt about Ollie. Tonight was her free pass. Her chance to let her guard down and take everything she wanted from him and she wasn't going to hesitate to drink every drop of this moment.

The way he'd lifted her and carried her to the bed had been exciting and turned her on more than she'd expected. Even though she'd come in the car she was hot and ready for him to be inside of her. She felt aching and empty without him as he was over her. His expression was intense, and their eyes met and something passed between them. Her heart beat heavier and he leaned down until their foreheads rested against each other. She felt the tip of him at the entrance of her body and then he entered her, driving into her with one long thrust. He was big, bigger than she'd anticipated, and he filled her completely. She threw her head back. His mouth took hers, his tongue rubbing over hers as he pulled his hips back and thrust into her again.

She opened her legs wider, digging her heels into the bed and thrusting upward, trying to take more of him. His mouth moved down her neck and she felt him at her breast, sucking her nipple into his mouth while he continued driving into her.

She rotated her hips so that her clit rubbed against him each time he drove into her and she felt herself getting closer to her climax. She put her hands on the back of his neck, drawing his head up to hers, sucking his tongue deep into her mouth as she felt her orgasm break over her and lights danced behind her closed eyes.

Ollie shifted, his hand going under her butt and lifting her hips so he could drive deeper into her, which just prolonged her orgasm. She felt him driving harder and faster into her until his body jerked and he called her name. He buried his face in her shoulder, thrusting into her a few more times before he settled into her arms and rolled to the side, keeping their bodies joined.

He held her loosely to him, sweat dried on their bodies, and she curled into his side. She rested her head on his shoulder and that tattoo he hadn't wanted to discuss was right there over his heart. She tried to ignore it and keep quiet and just enjoy the moment.

He lifted his head and turned to her. "You good?"

"Yeah. Bit better than good," she admitted. "You know how to give a cowgirl a good ride."

"Thank you, ma'am. I've got to clean up. Want something to drink?"

She nodded as he climbed out of the bed and she

watched his naked body as he moved toward the bathroom. She saw the strength in him, the scars on his back from where he'd been gored by a bull a time or two.

She shifted around on the bed, propping the pillows up behind her and getting under the sheets. He went to the mini bar. "What can I get you?"

"I don't know but take your time. I'm enjoying the view," she said. He stood there flexing his back muscles and butt cheeks until she was laughing.

Then he bent down and got them both water and some snacks and came back to the bed. He took some pillows and shoved them behind him and then put his arm around her and hauled her closer to his side.

He kissed the top of her head. "I know you got questions."

She did, but she took her time, took a long sip of her water and then wondered why she needed to know. Was it going to make her love him more or less if she knew the details of his past? She had no clue. But that tattoo was niggling around her mind and she wanted to know what had made him get it.

"So the tattoo you didn't want to forget. What does it mean to you?" she asked.

He sighed, put his head back against the headboard, just staring up at the ceiling and she thought he was going to answer her at first but then he put his water bottle on the nightstand and shifted so that their eyes met.

"It means that I don't have a heart and I need to remember that," he said.

"What? We all have a heart. And if you mean yours has been broken…Is that what you mean?" she asked. She was pretty sure that was what he meant. Probably it was tied to Mia and she hadn't yet decided if she wanted to know about her. She wasn't sure she wanted to talk about her own past. And if they were going to bare their souls, both of them had to do it.

It wouldn't be fair otherwise and Colby was all about fair.

"Nope. It means I don't have a heart, and I have to be careful not to break anyone else's."

She shook her head. "That sounds like there is a whole story in there."

He nodded but didn't say anything else.

She wasn't going to ask again. He was evasive and maybe that was okay. She'd taken the lead tonight, taken what she'd always wanted from him, and it was beyond her dreams but this…this might be something he couldn't do. He might still be thinking she was just here until Nico's wedding.

Which was what they'd agreed to so why did it hurt so much at this moment?

Chapter Twelve

*I*T MEANS *I don't have a heart.*

Those words had been his truth for so long that he hadn't questioned them until he was holding Colby in his arms. But then he remembered the destruction he'd caused with Mia and that feeling. That helplessness. He'd vowed to never feel that way again. And everyone agreed he was a man of his word.

She had questions; he could see them in her eyes. But he could avoid them, roll over and go to sleep. Colby probably wouldn't let him get away with that. But he knew that things would never be the same between them again. He was at a damned crossroads again. He had a choice and like that moment he'd asked her to be his temporary fiancée, he had to either man up or walk away.

And he wasn't walking away.

This was no different than facing down a crazy bull that no one wanted to draw. He could handle it. It wasn't managing tough situations he couldn't handle, it was the aftermath.

"What are you thinking? I swear you look like you wanted to smile," she said.

She'd drawn the sheet up to cover her breasts and watched him cautiously. Gone was the sexy, sensual woman who had set his body and soul on fire.

"I was comparing this situation to a tough bull," he admitted.

She raised her eyebrows. "Am I the bull?"

"Maybe," he said. "Listen, I guess there is a reason why I favor one-night stands with buckle bunnies at the rodeo."

"Duh," she said. "There's a reason I keep to myself."

"I figured," he said. "I want to hear about that, but before I can ask you to share something that personal, I want you to know exactly what you are dealing with."

"Did you kill someone?"

"No," he said, shocked. "Never. Why would you ask me that?"

"You're being too serious. I know that you were hurt and probably hurt Mia. But that's life. I don't like it any more than you do but we all get hurt. Love's like that. We don't get to choose who we do or don't fall for. It happens and then…we deal with the fallout. Sometimes it's like my parents or your parents and it just really clicks. The universe smiles and all is right."

She turned and leaned back against the headboard, pulling her legs up to her chest and resting her cheek on it as she turned to face him. "Tell me."

Tell her.

After that he wasn't sure he could. She had been so right and the pain in her voice when she'd said we don't chose who we love...it had cut him deep. Who did she love that hadn't loved her back? What man would do that to Colby? He knew he was letting himself get distracted by wanting to defend her. Avoidance. He knew it well.

"So I've always been a pretty open guy. In college I started dating Mia. She was a lot of fun, seemed to match my dream of life. I wasn't committed to going into business like my father, but Mia thought it would be a good idea and I didn't really hate it. Jock wasn't going to take over the business and Nico had already started making a name for himself in brand management. But the Rossis have been importer/exporters forever and she and I thought that I might enjoy doing it."

"You in an office all day? I can't see it."

He smiled at her. She was so right. "Back then I was caught up in a version of myself that Mia saw and that my family wanted for me. I started to believe they might be right. We got engaged our junior year."

"So I'm not your first fiancée?" she asked.

He shook his head. She wasn't but somehow this fake engagement felt more real to him. Maybe it was because with Colby he felt more comfortable being himself. "Mia...things sort of changed after we got engaged. Mia seemed different. Our life was no longer this thing that we were both planners and participants in. She had a new vision for us. I tried to keep up but the more plans she made for our life together the less it felt like our life."

"What did she want that you didn't?" she asked.

"I'm not sure I can pinpoint it. But she mapped out the neighborhood where we should buy our first house, where we should go on our vacations, when we should have kids… The more she talked about our life together, the more I realized I didn't want that life. I had started my internship at Rossi Import/Export and didn't love it as much as we'd expected me to."

She turned to face him, still keeping the sheet over her breasts. "So everything was changing and none of it was what you wanted?"

"Exactly. I did try to talk to Mia, but she was on the bride/wedding train and it was a high-speed one. She just didn't hear what I was saying. I talked to my father, told him I had doubts about the job and the wedding, and he said all men get nervous. I think he's right in a way. I let him know I wanted to try other careers," Ollie said.

His father had been very supportive about that but had asked him to keep working with Rossi Import/Export while he explored other options. He knew that the family business wasn't for everyone and he'd told Ollie that in time he would be happier.

He'd had a similar conversation with Mia and let her know that he wasn't sure they were on the right path. He had been thinking of taking the last semester of their senior year off to figure some stuff out. She was a little concerned but at the time Ollie thought that he needed to figure out his own life before he started one with Mia.

"I took off with the rodeo after a talk with Mia. Learned clowning from Dusty and loved it. I didn't expect to. I came back for Mia's graduation and I realized how much we'd grown apart at the party at her parents' place. I told her and she didn't really understand what I was saying. She said once we were married everything would sort itself out."

"But it didn't?"

"Huh?" he asked, remembering the tears in Mia's eyes and the pain he'd caused both of their families.

"Your marriage didn't work out?"

"Uh, no. I broke the engagement at her party. Told her that we weren't going to sort it out because we were different people and wanted different things from life. I hadn't realized that everyone had gotten quiet. She asked me if I still loved her and I answered honestly that I wasn't sure I ever had."

Tin Man.

She could think of a million justifications to explain what had happened between him and Mia but at the same time she could see that Ollie was showing her the man he believed himself to be. He'd found peace with the woman he'd hurt and the life that he'd left behind.

"You've always been honest," she said.

Because she had the feeling he wanted her to say something. But what could she say? She loved this man and that story made her love him even more. Which made her wonder if she was just letting her emotions run away because he'd pretty much guaranteed that he'd never be able to return them. She'd been hurt. She wasn't going to lie about that. Her story wasn't anything like his, but the pain was still there. And there was a part of her that wanted the big romantic love that pervaded the stories she adored.

The kind of epic love that maybe Mia had thought she had with Ollie when she'd planned her dream wedding and life. Colby was beginning to wonder if it even really existed or if she'd just set herself up for something that would never happen.

"I try. But the truth is I don't want to hurt anyone like I hurt Mia again. It was more than just Mia, but her parents and mine. Our families were good friends," he said.

That had to have made it harder. "You could have just kept quiet and married her and lived that dream life she planned and been miserable and probably made her unhappy too."

She wanted to see the silver lining. To see this honesty as something noble but in the back of her mind was the feeling that maybe he'd run away from commitment. Maybe settling down wasn't in the cards for him.

"I could have. I thought about it. But I wanted her to

find a guy who could be that excited about the life she was dreaming of with her. In a way she'd shown me something that I wanted to find, but it wasn't with her."

Something he wanted to find.

"So you believe in love?"

"Not sure. I'll tell you since we broke our engagement, I haven't met anyone who'd made me want to commit…until I asked you to be my fake fiancée."

She swallowed. *Be cool, girl.* She couldn't read too much into the fact that he'd said everything she'd always wanted to hear. "And?"

He turned to face her, that big, muscled chest of his bare, the tattoo over his heart that she knew he wasn't detached from no matter how much he might be telling her that he could feel again.

"Well you know I like you. I said I wanted to date you, Colby-girl. You are making me feel things that I didn't think I could. I'm afraid to even contemplate the future because what if this is the only part that I'm good at? The excited falling for each other phase?" he said.

Honesty.

Again.

And it was so much more than she'd expected from him. "I am not sure either. I've never fallen for a man who liked me back. It's always been sort of one-sided. Love from afar."

"Like you said we can't control who we fall in love with. Who did you love?" he asked.

How could she tell him the truth and not let him see that she was already in love with him? She chewed her lower lip, hating that when it came to her emotions, she could never be real. She was so blunt and honest about everything else but when it came to this…

She was vulnerable and she hated that.

She'd always been a tough cowgirl. Her daddy had always said he was proud of that about her and she'd liked it. She wasn't like her sister who cried when she fell off her horse or had big dramatic fights with her boyfriends, who easily loved and wore every emotion on her sleeve.

Nope, not her. Not the tough cowgirl.

"High school I was in love with the star quarterback who was happy enough for me to tutor him in English but never asked me out."

"High school doesn't really count. You were too young. What man made you believe that you only love the ones who don't love you?" he asked.

He was demanding like for like with the truth he'd shared with her and she wasn't going to let him down.

"I started riding professionally after high school. Met a bronco rider, and we really hit it off. We started living together and I fell hard for him. But when the rodeo broke for the summer, I thought we'd spend it together and he told me he had a girlfriend back home. That our thing was just for the rodeo. You'd think that would make me hate him…" She trailed off and shrugged.

She wasn't going to admit that she'd thought about telling Billy that she'd be happy with just the rodeo summers together. She'd thought he was the perfect man for her. She'd built their rodeo life into something that felt all-consuming. If it hadn't been for her sister who'd told her to snap out of it. That she deserved better than a part-time man...

"It didn't," Ollie said. "You deserve more than a summer lover, Colby-girl. You deserve so much more than that."

"More than a fake fiancé?" she asked, immediately regretted it but she couldn't pull the words back. It wasn't a text she hadn't hit send on, he was sitting right there, and the words were just the natural extension of the honesty that he'd brought to their bed.

But at the same time, she wished she'd kept them to herself.

OLLIE DIDN'T BLAME her for asking that question. He'd been thinking about it since...well since they'd arrived at her parents' house one day ago. Why had temporary fiancée been the thing he'd thought of? He hadn't wanted to be engaged again after Mia but Colby... Well it was like having his cake and eating it too. He'd get his mom off his back and he'd have finally been able to ask her out.

Wait, what?

He hadn't thought of her as a girl until that ride. When

he'd kissed her on the picnic blanket with Shep nearby and he'd realized how beautiful she was. How he'd missed it before that moment he couldn't say.

"Yes," he said. "That's why I've changed the dynamic as soon as I could."

"Did you?" she asked.

"You know you're the one who wanted to just be friends," he reminded her gently.

He could admit that he wasn't in a place to have fully appreciated Colby five years ago when they'd first met, but she'd pretty much friend-zoned him from the first, which made sense given what he now knew of her past and the idiot she'd thought she loved. But she hadn't been any more ready for him than he'd been for her. His honesty made her very aware that she was lying to him and maybe a little bit to herself. It had been safer loving him at a distance and a part of her had reveled in the safety of it.

She exhaled with a long sigh. "You're right. I hate to admit—"

"That I'm right? It's okay I am a lot," he teased, because he didn't want to keep talking about the past and the mistakes they'd both made. He was in bed with Colby and he felt some hope for a future with her. That was huge for him and he wanted to enjoy every single second of it.

"You are so arrogant. You're not right nearly as often as you think you are," she pointed out.

"Like when?"

"Like…" She trailed off and he could see her thinking.

"Like when I asked you to be my fiancée from March until June and then kissed you and it was hotter than a Texas summer?"

She gave him a tight smile, but he knew he had her with that. "Maybe. But I'm pretty sure you had no idea it would be that hot."

She was right. If he had he would have been on her way before this year. How had he missed the attraction that was there between them? The attraction that had been growing since he'd asked her for this favor. An attraction that in no way was forced or faked and was teasing him with the idea of what it could lead to.

But he had to trust himself. He had to believe that once he really let this be more than a fling, that it would last.

Because as much as he knew that Mia's plans had made him feel trapped, he knew it had been more than that. It had been the job, the staying in one place, the life that he knew his parents loved but that had never really appealed to him.

And it wasn't as if Colby was saying he had to get an office job and move to a house in the suburbs…in fact, he had no idea what she wanted. Maybe that was for the best. Or was it another form of running away?

"What are you thinking about?" she asked. "You have a very serious look on your face."

"Just wondering if this fake engagement was another form of me—never mind. Want to cuddle and try to think of more times I was right?" he asked. But he knew that he'd changed the dynamic again. He'd said what he was really thinking and there was no going back from it.

Colby wasn't the kind of woman to back down and she didn't disappoint now. "Wondering if you were running away again?"

Damn.

He wished that she were a little less honest. That just once when it came to the tough stuff she'd flinch or look away. But that wasn't her way and he knew that was probably why he liked her so much.

"Yeah."

"I'm wondering if I'm falling for another man who is going to never love me back, Tin Man. Have I screwed up again when it comes to me?" she asked.

"No. This isn't on you. You haven't screwed up at all. I'm the one who—"

"We are both here. We both agreed to a temporary serious relationship. I think we have to ask ourselves why. What do we both want from this?"

She was right. He hadn't thought what she might want from him that he wasn't giving her. In fact, until she'd said that, he hadn't realized that her past was also very entwined with this fake fiancée thing.

"I want you, Colby. That's it. I thought I wanted my mom to stop setting me up and to not have to dread coming home alone. But somehow that changed. Maybe it was between the rodeo and Georgetown or between Georgetown and Whiskey River, but somewhere it did. I can't go back to whatever was motivating me before because now it is tied to you."

She chewed her lip again and then threw herself into his arms. He wrapped his around her and held her close. "I hope that's true, Ollie, because you're the reason I'm here. I think you might have been the only man who could have asked me to do this and I'd have said yes."

He rubbed his hands up and down her back, lowering his head to kiss her. They made love again and this time when it was over, they both drifted off to sleep in each other's arms. He told himself that he was lucky to have found a woman like Colby and that he believed this could work out.

But he felt a stone weight in his stomach, and he was afraid of how this might end with him hurting the one woman he'd let back into his life after so long alone.

Chapter Thirteen

COLBY WOKE TO the smell of coffee and the sound of Ollie singing off-key in the shower along with "Whatcha Gonna Do With A Cowboy"—the duet with Garth Brooks and Chris LeDoux. After last night it was exactly what she needed to hear this morning.

She hopped out of bed, took a sip of the coffee and then went into the bathroom, which was steamy from his shower. He smiled at her when he saw her. The bathroom had a large rain shower on one end and a claw-foot tub on the other and a long double vanity in between.

"Whatcha gonna do with this cowboy?" he sang to her.

"I think I might keep him," she said. "If he gets me some breakfast while I'm showering."

"Yes, ma'am. Want to join me in here? There's plenty of room," he invited.

"Yes. But I have to brush my teeth first," she said. She hated the way her mouth felt in the morning and always had to brush her teeth first. She brushed her teeth and got in the shower where he waited for her.

"Thought I'd help you out with the washing," he said.

"You're so thoughtful," she said, but had to laugh because the only parts he wanted to wash were her boobs and butt. Soon they were running their hands over each other and he had her pinned to the tile wall as he slid inside of her and whispered good morning.

Sex was fast and deep and he pulled out when he came, which she had to admit she appreciated but another part of her wished they were the real couple he thought they were on the path to being, so he didn't have to.

He kissed her long and deep. "Colby-girl, you make me a better man. I'll leave you to finish up and go order us some breakfast. Eggs and all the fixings?"

"Yes, please," she said.

He toweled off and left her alone in the bathroom. As soon as she did, she leaned against the tile wall, her pulse still racing, her body still pulsing from his and her mind unable to focus on the truth.

She was more in love with Ollie than she'd ever been and she wasn't sure he was any closer to falling in love with her. Only a fool would discount the fact that he'd told her that he wasn't sure he could care for her beyond this phase of the relationship.

And she wasn't a fool.

Really, she thought. She took her time in the shower, knowing she needed the time to herself to get her head on straight. She washed her hair and then when she got out, blow-dried it with the one the hotel had supplied and then she put on the robe also supplied by the hotel. She heard the knock on the outer door and Ollie directing room service where to set up their breakfast and she knew she had to go out.

Go out there and be cheerful and not let him see how she really felt about him. But she had to seem like she was starting to really like him. This was so convoluted in her mind that she just shook her head.

This was probably why she was going to lose him. She either had to drop the façade altogether or…what?

There was no *or*.

She loved him. She was with him for now and had this chance to prove to herself she was worthy of his love.

There.

That was what she'd been afraid to admit she wanted.

Her fear. That she would admit she loved him, and he'd walk away.

Hell, he'd already told her that he had walked away from the last woman who loved him.

He'd gotten a freakin' tattoo to remind himself not to do it again.

And here she was—

"Hey, you okay in there? Food's here."

She opened the door and forced a smile but she knew he wasn't fooled.

"I'm fine."

"No, you're not. What's up?" he asked.

"I'm just trying to figure out if I should be chill and act like last night was just like any other or be...well honest and let you know that it changed things between us," she said. "Guess I made that choice."

He touched the side of her face. "I'm glad you did. I can't hide how happy I feel today, Colby. Last night did change things and I'm just going to enjoy the ride. What about you?"

Enjoy the ride.

She could do that. For now. But she knew eventually she was going to want to get off the ride and walk into the sunset or sunrise to something permanent. But for now, she'd go with it. This was more than she'd expected to find when she had agreed to this crazy idea of his.

So much more.

"Sounds about right. I just don't want to scare you off," she admitted as they moved into the main suite to the table, which was set for breakfast.

"Me either," he said. "I think as long as both of us are honest we should be fine."

Honest.

Sure. That worked. As long as she was able to keep the fact that she loved him to herself until he figured out if he could love her or not in return.

Which felt dishonest but she shoved that aside. For once she wasn't going to worry about that. She wasn't going to look to the future and let it scare her into hiding. She was going to take this chance with him and love him until he had no choice but to love her back.

She ignored the little voice in the back of her head that reminded her that she couldn't make him love her.

She didn't want to face that truth. Not now. Soon enough she'd know if this gamble she'd taken had paid off or if she'd made the worst mistake of her life.

OLLIE HADN'T PLANNED on spending any extra time in Whiskey River but when Colby had suggested they check out the shops on Main Street, well, he realized she didn't want to return to their regular life. This weekend was too short, and he knew he didn't want it to end.

"Booze Kelly must have been a character," she said, as they paused by the plaque that told his story near the river path. There were footbridges that were also part of the path and the river was running high as it was spring but not so high so as to endanger the town.

"From what I've heard of the Kelly family they all are," Ollie said. "Nicholas and his brother Zander didn't even know they were related to Boots Kelly until he died. That's legit not normal."

She laughed. "Like pretending to be engaged?"

He laughed with her. "Yeah. But we have good reasons for that. You know I sort of like that we have this thing that only we know."

She tipped her head to the side, studying him the way she did when she wasn't sure if he was telling her the truth or not. "I like it too."

There was a hesitation in her voice. "But?"

"But...I just feel like this entire thing has gotten away from both of us. What I intended in the beginning, what you did. I mean we are hell and gone from there as my daddy likes to say."

They were hell and gone from that. He was on a slippery path and the rodeo clown in him liked it. The danger of not knowing what was coming next, the adrenaline of knowing that whatever it was he'd be pushed to the max. Then there were these feelings she stirred in him, the way that he wasn't exactly sure what they were and the fear of identifying them.

He cursed under his breath, took her hand in his and started them walking again. The crisp spring breeze blew around them with a hint of warmth, promising a taste of summer and what was to come. That's all he wanted from her. Some warmth, a hint of what was their future. But life didn't work like that. He had no way of knowing if Colby was as different to him as she felt or if she was just the first real woman, he'd let himself know since Mia.

That was it.

He was afraid.

He didn't want to hurt Colby or himself. And the man who could face down bulls without breaking a sweat was suddenly afraid. Afraid of emotions and what they could do to a man. How love could be the most exquisite feeling in the world and the most devastating. They came to a bridge that led back to the Square and he started to turn but she stopped him.

"Are you going to ignore what I said?" she demanded.

He had been lost in trying to figure out what to say to her. This was a side that he knew he liked about Colby but at the same time didn't. She was stubborn. Any other woman would have let it go. He wished she would. But she wasn't any other woman. She was Colby and…damn!

"Yes. I was, but now I can't, can I?"

"You can if you want to drive back to Georgetown with a pissed woman in the cab of your truck."

"Could I soften you up with some of those cookies we smelled baking in the shop earlier?" he asked. Still hedging and dodging—it was his instinct when he saw trouble coming to divert, amuse, save his skin.

"No. I want the truth. I feel like I'm riding around the barrels and I can feel that my cinch is loose and I'm not sure I'm going to stay in the saddle until the end of my ride," she admitted. "We're supposed to be friends. I expect…well better of you."

He shook his head, dropped her hand and turned away. Looking up the river at the current pushing the water swiftly down beneath the bridge. He wanted to jump in and let it carry him away. But he had decided not to run this time. Not to dodge either Colby or this thing… Had he decided?

It felt like he was wobbling. And that pissed him off because he wasn't a wobbler by nature. He was sure, confident, some would say arrogant but screw them. He knew he was. Why was he suddenly unsure?

Those damned emotions no doubt.

"I've got you, Colby-girl. I'm here with you. I don't know what's what either, but you're not alone. This isn't what either of us planned, but I for one like where we are," he said.

She nodded and put her hand on his forearm. "I like it too. I'm just not sure where it ends."

Did she think he was?

"The future isn't written," he said. "We only have the present."

That was all he could give her. It was all he could give himself. If it wasn't enough for her, then he didn't know what he'd do next. But that was life. He'd roll with it and sort it out.

"The present. I guess that's all we need to worry about right now," she said. "Well and if they are going to have enough of those cookies left for both of us."

He slipped his hand back into hers and they walked over the footbridge. He talked about cookies and sweets and pretended that everything had been resolved but he knew, and he suspected she did too that nothing had.

They were both still in the middle of something and neither of them was sure where they wanted to be. A better man would cut her free. Let her find a straightforward relationship that wouldn't put her in this turmoil. But she was his now. After last night, cutting her lose wasn't something he was willing to contemplate. Not now and maybe not ever.

COLBY WAS GLAD when they left Whiskey River, then stopped at her folks' house just long enough to hook up the horse trailers and get into their own vehicles. She hugged Shep when she saw him. The one man to never let her down.

"He missed you," her dad said.

"Missed him too. Did he eat?" she asked.

"A little but not much. He hates when you're away."

She rubbed her silly dog. "I'm always coming back to you, boy. Eat when I'm not around—it's okay."

He made a grumbling sound and just rubbed his snout against her neck and suddenly she felt overwhelmed by her emotions, like she was going to start crying. She put her head on Shep and wished that love with men was as easy as it was with her dog. He always was happy to see her; he wanted nothing from her than this. Cuddles, food, company.

Was it too much to ask that Ollie would want the same from her?

Well for more than a few months or however long he saw this lasting. She guessed he'd gone ahead and told her that he didn't look ahead and maybe that was for the best. After all the last time he'd committed to a woman he'd ended up leaving not only the woman but his life behind as well.

That wasn't the man she knew, and she knew it had been at least five years since he'd done that, but at the same time, the risk she'd taken was getting higher. The stakes were ones she was no longer sure she wanted to risk.

It was one thing to toy with making him fall in love with her but this was something else.

She felt a hand on her shoulder. "You okay, girl?"

Her daddy's sweet, deep voice. Full of concern and a little bit of reluctance as he didn't like to see any of his girls cry. "Yeah, just tired. It was a long weekend."

She got to her feet, wiping her hands on the back of her jeans. "Thanks for watching Shep."

"Anytime. Mama said to tell you we are going to come and see you in Oklahoma City," he said. "You need anything before you head out?"

"No. Thanks, Daddy," she said, hugging her father.

She noticed Ollie walking toward them and she sighed. What was she going to do with him?

"Give him hell, Colby. Don't forget you're a Tucker."

She laughed. Her daddy always knew the right thing to say. "I intend to."

"That's my girl," he said, before walking over to Ollie.

Colby took Shep for another potty break while her dad and Ollie chatted and then she got the dog in the cab of her truck and leaned against the driver door, waiting for Ollie to finish talking. He strolled over to her as her dad gave her a final wave and went back into the house.

"Everything okay?" he asked her.

"Yeah. Why?"

"Just saw your dad hug you… Seemed like…well I know it's been more than you bargained for and no matter what impression I might have given you, I care about you."

She sighed and shook her head. "I know. Sometimes I think it might be easier if you didn't."

"Yeah?" he asked. "I guess I haven't given you a good impression of me caring about a woman. But I'm not the man I once was."

"And I'm no longer that girl," she said. But the truth was she wasn't that confident of that fact. She was still longing for a man who didn't love her. And this time she wasn't sure that she should be. Sleeping with him, spending the day with him had given her a glimpse of a life she wanted.

Something more than just the present but he wasn't there yet. He might never be there and she knew that.

She had to face that.

"I'll follow you again," she said, trying to end this conversation before the mania in her head spilled out and she just told him the truth that was harder and harder for her to hide.

"Yeah. That works. I need gas so we'll have to stop first."

Mundane, normal, everyday details that couples discussed. That's what this felt like. How many times had her parents had this very conversation? It was hard not to let it feel like more. She wanted to draw a connection between the two of them and other couples she knew but couldn't.

"There's a station just up the road. Want to follow me there?"

"Sounds good," he said, starting to turn away before abruptly reaching for her and pulling her into his arms. He kissed her long and hard and all of a sudden, she wasn't sure about anything. That kiss made her feel…well like he might be closer to loving her than she'd thought he was.

He set her back on her feet and then stalked to his truck and she watched him get in, bringing her hand to her lips. What did that mean?

Was she ever going to really know what was going on in his head? She was beginning to seriously doubt it. She got in the cab of her truck and drove to the gas station, parking up away from the pumps while Ollie filled up his tank.

She sat there and the song playing was "Crazy" by Patsy Cline and she shook her head and pushed the button to change the station. Not in the mood for any kind of karmic intervention. She didn't want this love to be crazy. She wanted it to be the forever kind that George Strait liked to sing about. She wanted to know that she'd made the right choice but knew there was no easy answer.

No way of knowing for sure until it was all over. Until his brother got married and Ollie either walked away or decided to stay.

She felt powerless and trapped by her own decisions and her own foolish heart.

Chapter Fourteen

I T HAD BEEN two weeks since they'd gone to Whiskey River. The rodeo was winding its way through the southwest, joining up with the bigger PBR shows when it could and hitting small towns most weeks. They'd camped in a large field that had once been a homestead but was abandoned decades ago. There was a decent-sized barn that the rodeo had reinforced and most of them were camped in the field close to it. Colby had lit off on her horse a few hours ago and he'd watched her leave as he'd headed to the ring for the practice rides.

Something had been different between them since he'd stopped for gas after leaving her folks' place. She was still doing her part, being his fake fiancée, talking to his parents and sister when they called. She was even friendly and affectionate with him, but she'd made excuses whenever he tried to get back into her bed.

Excuses and Colby were two things that truly never went together, not in his mind. And as clueless as he could be to what she was actually thinking, it didn't take a genius to figure out she was ticked at him.

But why? That part was a mystery. He sort of figured it was the way he'd told her he could only live in the moment. It had to be that. Like what else could it be? But would she have rather he lied to her?

Lying wasn't his thing. He wouldn't let it be. So when he was done with practice and had changed out of his clown gear and she still wasn't back, he knew he had two choices. Didn't a man always? But for him it was troll for buckle bunnies or go find the one woman he wanted to make peace with.

He saddled up his horse and headed out toward a copse of trees that he'd noticed when they'd driven up to the camping site. He wanted to say that she was drawing him to her, but he wasn't that fanciful, and he knew that was the sort of place she would have headed.

Shep was with her and the dog liked a good run and then to hunt for a stick to play with. He hated this distance between the two of them and for the first time as he rode and searched for her, he realized that this was what it would be like after Nico's wedding.

Or would it?

He had no idea what she really wanted from him for the future. She hadn't said just asked him where he saw them. And because he was an arrogant ass at times, he'd never thought to ask her where she saw them. What did she think the next step was?

His knees ached as he finally spotted her lying on the top

of a rolling hill. She had her head propped up against her saddle and as he got closer he saw she was reading a book. Shep had his head on Colby's thigh and his paw on a branch that was longer than he was.

She glanced over as he got off the horse and dropped the lead to the ground, knowing his horse would stay. He walked over to her but stopped, not sure of his welcome. He opened up his saddle bags and took a thermos of peach iced tea and two chocolate brownies that he'd made the night before. His brother had sent him the recipe and told him it was fool-proof.

Here's hoping.

"Mind if I join you?" he asked.

She held her finger up and continued reading, flipping the page and then tucking a leather bookmark into the book and closing it. "Not at all. But I'm feeling lazy so you might find it boring."

"I doubt that very much." He sat down on the blanket next to her and took a carrot from his pocket for Shep. Tossing it on the blanket next to the dog.

Shep went for his treat as Colby sat up, tossing her hair with her hand. "What'd you bring for me?"

"Peach iced tea and homemade brownies."

She raised both eyebrows at him. "Who'd you get to make them?"

"No one. I did it myself," he admitted. "Never baked before and even though Jock assures a child could make these, I'm not sure."

"You haven't tried them?"

He opened the Ziploc container and set it between the two of them as he poured some iced tea into the cups he'd brought as well. "Nope. What if they were bad and I got sick and I was by myself?"

"So you wanted to try them with a witness in case of emergency?" she asked him drily.

"Seemed sensible."

"Which is totally not you," she said. "I'll try one first though just in case. I feel like you have a better shot of lifting me than I do lifting you. If you kick it I'm going to have to drag you back to camp on this blanket."

"No one is going to kick it. I didn't put anything weird in the brownies."

She shook her head and laughed at him. "I know."

She took one of the brownies and took a tentative bite and he waited to see if she liked them. She took a second bite and still didn't say anything. After she'd finished off the square she wiped her hands and gave him a serious look. "Not bad, but I don't want you to be disappointed so I probably should eat the rest."

She was teasing him and for the first time since they'd gotten back to the rodeo, he felt like things might be okay between them. "You're a good friend to make such a sacrifice, but I think I should at least try one."

"Fair enough but don't say I didn't warn you."

"I won't," he said.

He took a bite and the brownies were pretty good. Jock had come through with the recipe and his cooking advice. And he'd never let his brother know it, but he might have helped him get back on track with Colby.

COLBY HAD BEEN letting things ride since they'd returned. Harder than she would have thought it would be, but it had felt right. She was letting herself start to fall more into love with Ollie and that hadn't felt healthy.

She was reminding herself very much of the woman she'd been with Billy and she refused to go back down that route. She remembered the promise she'd made to herself when she'd come back to the rodeo and before Ollie had come to her camper. She couldn't stay in this exquisite torment that was unrequited love. Not anymore. She had shown Ollie the real woman she was.

But here she was flirting and laughing with him while eating brownies that were way better than anyone's first attempt at baking should be. But then this was Ollie. He was a master at anything he wanted to be.

So why had love eluded him. What had scared him so much that he'd run away from his future and his fiancée? Sure, he could say it was that they grew apart but something had made him run.

Beckett had said that some men were too much of a lone

alpha wolf to ever become part of domestic life. But she couldn't see it. Was that where Ollie was?

"Thanks for eating these with me," he said.

"Thanks for sharing. How'd practice go?"

"Not bad. My knees are starting to get a bit tetchy on the first day. I'll deny this if you repeat it, but I might be getting too old to rodeo."

"Oh, ho. Much too young to feel that damn old?" she sang the line from the Garth Brooks song. But she knew the feeling. Barrel racing wasn't as hard on the body as bull or bronc riding or even clowning, but it was still tough.

Plus being fake engaged had made her start thinking of the future. Too much. She did see a time when she had a home of her own. Something bigger than the camper—where she could raise horses and have a life. The only problem was that she wanted to see Ollie with her in that house. But she didn't feel comfortable asking him about it. Asking him where he saw himself.

She wasn't sure that she would be civil if he told her he saw herself in this moment again. She wanted to make plans, she wanted—

Hold up.

She was chill. She'd just spent the last two weeks learning to be chill where he was concerned and a few brownies and thirty minutes talking to him and she'd lost it all. She was hot for him. Not just his body, which looked better than it should as he sprawled next to her on the blanket.

His faded jeans that cupped him in all the right places, that plain white T-shirt he wore that clung to his pectorals and shoulders. The laugh lines around his eyes that crinkled whenever she said something that amused him.

She wanted to crawl over to him, curl up in his arms and tell him dreams of a future together.

And she couldn't. There was no way that he was even close to hearing that from her. He'd let her have these last two weeks. And that was a big red warning flag.

He was giving her the space she needed to keep doing what he wanted from her, but not making any promises.

Hell.

That was what he was good at. Giving her just enough to keep her hanging on and not making any commitments and she needed one.

She wanted one.

She was afraid to press him for one.

She knew it and she wasn't going to face that fear. Not today when the sun was in the sky, warming her skin, and he was lying so close watching her.

"What?" she asked as she realized he was staring at her.

"I missed you."

"I've seen you every day," she pointed out.

"Yeah, but you were distant. I hate that I might have ruined this for us. I don't want there to ever be a time when you and I can't laugh and be us."

Too late, she thought. That moment was gone long before he'd asked her to be his fake fiancée. She knew it had disappeared when she'd decided she couldn't keep up this one-sided love that she'd fallen into.

"I missed you too," she admitted. "I'm trying not to. I'm trying to just be in the moment but frankly, Ollie, that's not me."

He sat up and rubbed his hand on the top of his head, turning away from her to look toward the horizon. She wasn't sure what he was looking for. She had a feeling it wasn't the future.

"I don't want to make promises—"

"That you can't keep. I know. I have to ask you something and it's going to be uncomfortable. But it's the only way I'll know how to handle this. Did you run from your life because you don't want to be settled down? Are you afraid to grow old and stale or is it something else?"

"Well, damn, woman, don't hold back. Just ask for me to bare my soul," he said.

The harshness of his tone took her aback, but she wasn't backing down. She knew that she'd struck too close to the nerve. "Sorry but I'm falling for you and I'm not sure that I even really know you."

She didn't know what she wanted him to say but she knew she needed answers or explanations or even a placation. Like she was different, he wouldn't do that to her. Then she realized she didn't care if he lied to her and that hurt her more deeply than she'd thought it would because she realized how much of herself, she was willing to give away to him.

OLLIE SORT OF felt like the last two weeks had been leading to this. She'd been giving him time and waiting to see if he was going to run when he got bucked or hold on for the ride. Truth was, he didn't know the answer to her question. He'd kept life free and easy since Mia and it was only his mom's persistent matchmaking that had forced his hand.

The sky was clear and cloudless as he looked up, hoping for rain or a storm or something that would give him an excuse to avoid answering her. But the universe was telling him to stay where he was.

Stay.

The word echoed inside of his mind and he knew that it was probably because of the pretty brunette sitting next to him, waiting for him to prove he was willing to be her man.

Was he?

He wasn't ready to do this. Wasn't ready to face her and give her the answers she wanted. He didn't want to own up to the fact that living alone...was it working? He didn't know for sure. Partially because he had the best of both worlds when he was on the road. Colby for conversation and championship and the buckle bunnies for sex. But now that had changed. He didn't want the buckle bunnies and Colby was looking at him like the next few minutes were going to determine if she was still amiable to having him in her life.

But he pushed aside his own feelings, remembering earlier when he'd acknowledged that he hadn't taken her wants and needs into consideration. She'd said she was falling for him.

Falling for him how?

Love? Something less?

Falling for him.

Damn.

Okay. Man up, he thought. "I think I'm falling for you too."

She chewed her lip, and he was coming to realize how much he hated the fact that he made her do that. That he couldn't seem to say the right thing to keep her from doing that again and again. He wanted to say the words that would reassure her, not feed her doubts.

"Not the right thing to say?"

She shrugged and plucked at the blanket, concentrating on making little mountains of the fabric as if that was the most important thing at this moment. "I don't know."

When she spoke her voice was low and husky, full of suppressed emotion, and it made that stone in the pit of his stomach larger. He was hurting her. In a way that Mia had never been hurt, he realized, because Mia hadn't seen him. She'd seen them.

But with Colby there was no them. They were still very much their own individual silos. She was asking him to change that. To reach out and show her she wasn't alone.

He had to choke back his own doubts in himself and in them. He wanted to do this for her. And not just because he knew if he didn't that the last two weeks and the distance between them was going to be their new normal.

"I'm trying, Colby-girl, but the truth is I'm just as confused by this as you are. I didn't expect to find myself sleeping with my best friend or missing her in my bed. And I know that's not what you want. You want some reassurance or guarantee that I can make this last and screw it, you know I want that too. But I'd be lying to both of us if I made that promise to you."

She looked up at him, those big brown eyes so wide and serious that for a moment he was lost in them. Wanting to be the man she thought she saw in him but not sure he could be. It was the first time he'd felt his confidence take a hit with her. He'd been so damned sure that this was the right move. Now...

Who knew?

"I get it. I know I'm pushing you for something that is hard to admit to. But I just want to know that if let myself fall... What am I saying? There's no way I can stop it any more than you can promise that you won't break my heart."

She turned away and he reached out, stroked his hand down her arm and then lacing their fingers together. "I don't want to break your heart or mine. It might seem like my reticence is tied to me not caring, but that is not the truth."

"Reticence? I guess I can see your degree coming

through. You're still such a mystery to me, Ollie. I just need something solid to hold on to."

He tugged her off-balance and into his arms, lifting her onto his lap. She settled sideways and put her arm around his shoulder. She looked up at him and his heart started to beat faster in his chest. Something was changing and this time he didn't want to run away on his own. He wanted to scoop her up and take her someplace where the rest of the world would never find them.

"Hang on to me," he said, surprised at how gravelly his voice was. But he knew that was because he'd just realized how much this woman meant to him and that there was a very real chance that they might both end up with broken hearts.

She cuddled closer, her head resting on his shoulder as her arms tightened around him and they both held on as if they'd never let go, even though they both knew that wasn't true. They stayed in each other's arms for a long time and he knew that nothing had been resolved and that this was going to come up again, but they had found a fragile new peace and both of them seemed to be happy with that.

For now.

Chapter Fifteen

COLBY AND OLLIE fell into a pattern as they moved into May of living and working together. It was like every secret dream she'd ever had but never wanted to admit had come true. Ollie had left his camper in a lot near Dallas when they'd been there. He'd worked the big PBR show while she'd ridden in the smaller Mesquite rodeo.

Beckett and her husband Ash and their brood had come to watch her ride and afterward they'd met up with Ollie and gone to dinner. The entire night Colby had been on tenterhooks waiting to see if this family-ness was going to push Ollie away from her but he just pulled her close to him in the cab of the truck on the drive home and told her how much fun the evening had been.

Looking at him now as they were pulled into another weekend rodeo that looked pretty much the same as all the smaller ones, she almost let herself believe that this was going to work out. That he was falling for her and any moment now he was going to admit he loved her.

Almost.

Maybe she should take the first step and be the one to

tell him she loved him. But she couldn't. Didn't want to let her guard down that much and risk losing this. The few months they'd been together were some of her happiest and a part of her wanted to pretend this was enough.

She was too much a realist and if she were totally honest with herself too afraid to believe that this was going to work out better than she'd expected.

Ollie went to check in at the rodeo office while she took Shep for a walk and got the horses settled. When she came back her parents were chatting with Ollie. She was so happy to see them, she almost cried.

And that was her first clue that she was barely holding herself together. Her rides the last few rodeos had been better than she had expected, given that she sometimes woke up in the middle of the night to stare at Ollie and make sure he hadn't left.

As idyllic as the last few weeks had been, they were also an exquisite type of torture as well.

"Mama, Daddy! What are y'all doing here?" she asked as Shep tried to knock her dad over in greeting and her mama hugged her.

"I told you we'd come visit when you were back in Oklahoma City," she reminded her.

"I forgot. These last few weeks have been busy," she admitted. And they had been. Aside from seeing Beckett and her family in Dallas, Ollie's brothers Jock and Nico had come to visit and then Angelica had showed up unexpectedly. In fact looking back there hadn't been a rodeo where their families hadn't shown up.

"I bet you're looking forward to taking time off for the wedding," her mama said.

"I am," she admitted.

"Me too," Ollie said. "Maybe I can convince Colby to take an extra week and head to a secluded beach somewhere."

"Sounds like a good idea to me," her dad said.

"Well, we do have bills to pay," she pointed out. Well, she did. Ollie had plenty of money from his art and assorted other businesses that she was learning more about each week they were together.

"And she'd miss the rodeo if we weren't here," Ollie pointed out.

"True…and Shep isn't welcome at most resorts."

"Daddy and I will take Shep," her mama said.

"Great. When we figure it out, I'll let you know," she said to her mom. She didn't want to go on a vacation with Ollie until she knew that he cared for her as much as she did for him.

Work gave her a nice distraction from him and if they were all alone on a beach somewhere. She knew she'd have a hard time looking at anything but him. And then she'd get anxious about the unresolved emotions between them. That was it, she thought.

She wanted to pin him down and ask him if he cared for

her. Did he love her? Was he falling in love with her?

And she totally couldn't.

Which she knew and which was probably why she'd been freaking out and not really sleeping since they'd "moved in" together. She still didn't know what would happen after Nico's wedding. And she didn't have that much longer until she'd know.

Just two more weeks and then she'd have her answer.

If she didn't have a breakdown before then. No, she was too tough for a breakdown, but she didn't like this feeling. Not at all.

"When do you ride?" her mama asked as her father and Ollie were talking about the bulls provided by Blue and Powell.

"Tomorrow," she said to her mom. "I think it should be a good run. I've been on a winning streak."

"You're always on a winning streak," her mom said. "By the way, that cottage on Elm has come on the market. I know you have always loved that place. Want me and Daddy to go check it out and see if it's worth what they are asking?"

"Jasmine Cottage?" she asked. She'd spent so much time daydreaming that she lived in the 1890 cottage that was surrounded by blooming jasmine bushes, but since she'd moved away the elderly couple who lived there had let it fall into disrepair.

"The same. Mrs. Thomas can't take care of it on her own and her family are moving her back to Nashville," Mama said.

"I want it, Mama. If I can afford it. How much are they asking?"

Her mom told her, and Colby knew she could afford it. Her dream house was finally on the market. "It'll need updating."

"Yes," her mama said. "But you know Daddy and I will help you."

"Help you with what?" Ollie asked.

"Making Jasmine Cottage livable," she said. "My dream house has come on the market."

"Dream house? You've never told me about that. I thought this camper was your dream," he said.

She shook her head. "No. This camper is where I am now, but not where I want to be forever."

His face seemed to get tight, but he just nodded.

OLLIE WAS THE first to admit that the last six weeks had been both the best and worst of his life. He loved the time he and Colby had together with Shep. Driving between shows, sleeping and cooking together. Her lying on his lap and reading in their down time. These were the kinds of memories that he knew he was going to treasure forever.

But also they were inundated with way too many family visits. He got it. His family were so happy for him. His parents and Angelica had both told him so numerous times.

Jock and Nico were already talking about ski trips with "the women" over the winter ski season and at first, he was chill, but more and more it felt like his skin was too tight and he couldn't escape it.

Even making love to Colby had taken on a driven edge, like he was trying to assuage a hunger for her that would never be sated. He knew this.

Now her folks were here, and they were dear people. Both were great to talk to and they were treating him like...well, like a son. He got it. He had seen his parents do the same thing first to Delilah and then to Cressida. And to be honest they'd even treated Mia like a daughter way back when.

Somehow that just made the back of his neck itch and his eyes look to the horizon. Now the woman he was caring more and more deeply about by the day had a dream home.

A dream home?

Since when?

He hadn't heard her mention it in all the years he'd known her and surely if she'd wanted it for a while she would have brought it up. But she hadn't.

He knew this was what women did when they started thinking about forever. They found a home, they started building dreams and hopes around it and where did that leave him?

"You okay?" she asked under her breath as her mom went to get iced tea from inside the camper.

"Of course. Tell me about this place. What'd you call it…a cottage?"

She tipped her head to the side. "Jasmine Cottage. It's this 1890 house with two bedrooms and a big wooden porch around the front and side. It's got a tin roof and they planted loads of jasmine on the property so in spring when you drive by the smell is incredible. It's set on a big lot and there is a barn in the back. Room for a horse or two," she said.

It was clear to him that she was excited about the idea of this house and he could hear in her voice that this wasn't a new dream. Which reassured him. Slightly. "Near your parents' house?"

She nodded. "Closer to town than their place. The Thomases have owned it forever. But Mr. Thomas died last year, and his widow is moving out. I never thought the house would be on the market."

"How long have you liked it?" he asked. Trying to fit the pieces of this, trying to find something that would make him be able to chill out about her wanting to buy a house.

The house had nothing to do with him, but it was hard to see it that way right now. It felt like it was directly related to their growing relationship and he wanted to tell himself that it was okay, the next logical step.

But he hadn't been able to figure out if they'd be a couple after Nico's wedding. That was why he'd been so tired of their family dropping in. He was trying to figure out himself and Colby. Without the family pressure. It felt like it had with Mia. Everyone wanting to know their plans, everyone giving input—and yes, he was older and had his life...and somehow that made it harder for him to let go.

To just hop on this ride and follow where Colby led him.

That might be part of the probably. He wasn't a follower. Another part was that despite his aching knees, he wasn't ready to admit that he was done with clowning and the rodeo.

He knew that.

"Forever. I used to ride my bike past it when I was a girl and Mrs. Thomas—she was a friend of my grandma—used to invite me in for lemonade and then we'd work in her garden," Colby said.

Her words were the balm he hadn't wanted to admit he'd been looking for. She wasn't looking for a house because he was in her life or to settle down. She was clinging to a childhood memory and girlhood dreams.

"Do you think you'd be happy there now?" he asked. "You've changed a lot since then."

"I have," she said, nodding at him. "But that dream hasn't. Whenever I think of where I'll be when I stop touring with the rodeo, it's always at Jasmine Cottage. I know you live in the moment, but I can't stop looking to the future," she said.

"I know," he said. And he did know it. Deep inside he'd seen this coming for a long time. No matter how much he cared for Colby, they were two very different people and the friendship he'd cultivated with her over the last five years had shown him a woman who was very self-assured.

She knew herself and what she wanted. He was even more surprised than ever that she'd agreed to be his fake fiancée. Colby wasn't someone who'd do this—

Unless…

Did she want to be his real fiancée? Had she been…no. She couldn't have cared for him that way before this. She was too honest and too forthright to hide her feelings.

But he realized that he'd never really found out what it was that she'd wanted out of the fake fiancée thing. It wasn't to fool her parents because she'd told her sister straight out what was going on. And her sister had told their mom.

So what was it?

COLBY'S DAD HAD the grill on the fire when she and Ollie got back from the rodeo. Her mama had made her famous sangria and picked up sides at the Kroger on her way out of town. Ollie had been quiet since she'd mentioned Jasmine Cottage. She wasn't going to give up the chance to own her dream home for him. Was she?

She could tell it was putting extra pressure on their fragile relationship and she got it. She remembered him telling her how Mia had gone full-on planning the rest of their lives together the moment after he'd slipped that engagement ring on her finger. And this was different.

But how did she show him that it was without giving up the cottage?

She couldn't—wouldn't do that. The girl who'd been left behind by men before wasn't going to throw her future to one side on the off chance that he might stay.

Oh.

No.

Was this really where her head was?

Was she already saying goodbye to Ollie and they hadn't even been to his brother's wedding?

But she knew she was. That the fear that had been quietly lurking in the back of her mind during the last six weeks was now full on in her face. She'd seen it when she'd looked into those incredible blue eyes of his and found panic.

He might not call it panic but she knew what that looked like. She'd seen it in her own face when she'd tried to pretend that she could get over loving him. That being fake engaged was going to lead to anything other than heartache.

She'd lied to herself for too long.

And unless she wanted to up the ante and force his hand, she was going to have to either pretend she was giving up Jasmine Cottage or come clean with him and tell him she wasn't. She'd have to admit to loving him.

And it was at once the only thing she wanted to say to him and at the same time the one thing she never wanted to admit. She needed him to give her a clue he was falling for her, but Ollie played his emotions close to his chest.

Her parents left after they'd eaten, and she and Ollie put Shep in the camper as he built up the fire and pulled her onto his lap.

She took a deep breath, inhaling the scent of his after-shave, the feel of his strong arms around her and the way his profile looked silhouetted against the fire. He said nothing for a long time. She wasn't going to pretend that they both weren't still thinking of the future.

"You didn't say much about the cottage," she said at last. "I know you don't want me buying a house and picturing us living in it."

He looked down at her. "Don't I?"

"Please, don't be cute now. This is me being as serious as I can be with you."

"I'm trying. I don't want you to give up the cottage for me," he said. "Real estate is always a good investment."

"It is," she said. "But that's not why I want to buy it. I want it as my forever home. Where I raise horses and kids. I know you don't want to talk about the future, but I can't help it. When I think of Jasmine Cottage I see you sitting on the front porch swing next to me."

She held her breath subconsciously after she said that until she realized what she was doing and inhaled deeply and quickly.

"Well, hell."

Yeah. But it felt good to say it. To not skirt around what she wanted. Maybe she should have done this years ago. She couldn't have, but still she almost wished she would have. It felt freeing to say what she wanted.

"Also I can't keep this to myself any longer. I love you, Ollie Rossi."

He shifted his legs and she stood up before he did so he didn't dump her on the ground. He put his hands on his hips and then rubbed the top of his head the way he did. "You don't love me. It's the whole engagement thing making you believe that."

She shook her head sadly, thinking how little he knew her if he'd think she'd be confused about what she felt. "It's not. I loved you long before you asked me to do you a favor and be your fake fiancée."

"What? How long?" he asked.

His shock wasn't faked. She could tell he genuinely had no idea how she'd felt about him all these years.

"Since about two hours after we met the first time," she said.

"But you wanted to be friends," he pointed out.

"I didn't want to make another mistake like I had with Billy, and I'll tell you it wasn't long before I regretted that," she admitted.

He cursed under his breath. "I never knew... Why did you agree to be my fake fiancée?"

She swallowed because her hope that he'd fallen for her too was fading and fast. "I thought maybe you'd fall in love with me too."

She waited.

She'd put everything out there with that one statement.

He cursed again and then turned back to her. His hands on his hips and his gaze meeting hers. "That was a big risk to take."

"It was. But people in love do crazy things," she said. She hadn't realized just how much until this moment. She had finally told her crush, the man she'd fantasized about for what felt like forever how she felt, and he was just staring at her and not saying anything.

Well not saying the words she wanted to hear.

And it dawned on her slowly that he wasn't going to. He didn't feel it or couldn't admit it, but he wasn't going to tell her he loved her, and she had to face the fact that for Ollie this might have only ever been something temporary.

Chapter Sixteen

S HE LOVED HIM.

Having Colby's love wasn't something he'd expected. He was honest and knew that no one had ever called him the smartest Rossi and this evening was proving that nothing had changed recently. Colby wanted something from him. He admitted he wanted it himself, but he couldn't say the words she needed to hear. Couldn't do the one thing she needed him to.

He couldn't really identify why. Fear kept him from admitting he loved her. He didn't want to ask her to marry him for real and not be able to follow through. The last time when everything had seemed set it had rattled him to his core. And though he knew himself much better today than he had in the past, he was afraid to do anything to hurt Colby.

"Nothing? Really. You can't say anything to me?" She was angry and rightly so, but at the same time, he knew that it was a defense mechanism for her.

"I don't know what you want."

"Well, Ollie when a woman says she loves you, you

should at least acknowledge it."

"Thank you. I don't deserve your love. I'm not sure that I'm worthy of that, Colby. I've been trying for so long to figure out what I feel and why you make everything so different than it was before but…"

He trailed off. He didn't want to admit that he might not ever be able to love her. And now that he'd left his trailer, he had no place to stay but with her. They had both of their trucks as he was hauling both of their horses, but he had a feeling that tonight he wasn't going to be welcome in her bed.

"But you don't love me."

Blunt, forthright and strong as always, his cowgirl didn't pull any punches. "I don't know. I care about you very deeply and every day, spending time with you makes me happy."

"And you hate happy?"

"If you're just going to continue to snip at me then I'm not going to talk to you. I know I disappointed you, but I made you a promise to never lie and at this moment I can't tell you I love you. I'm not saying I don't but mentally I'm not there yet. And I know that's not romantic or sexy but that's who I am. If you need time to think, then I'll give it to you."

He turned away from her and away from the fire. All that beckoned him wasn't the horizon since it was pitch-dark and he couldn't see it. The only path was dark. He knew that. He hadn't wanted to do this tonight.

Sure, he'd felt the noose tightening when she'd mentioned a house. Buying a damned house. That was what she wanted. What she needed. What everyone wanted except him. Why?

He knew it was deeper than what had happened with Mia. And he still hadn't been able to face whatever it was.

"I'm sorry. I think...I've been walking on eggshells around you and trying to be what you need me to, but it's starting to weigh on me. I'm tired of not just saying I love you or making plans for the future. I know that you're not there and maybe if I were a smarter woman, I'd give you more time. But honestly, it feels like if I keep lying about how I feel a part of me is going to die," she said.

Her voice was low and husky. He heard the raw emotions and the sadness in it and cursed again because he wasn't sure what else to do. This was what he'd brought her to and it was difficult for him to see a way around it.

He glanced over his shoulder and wished he hadn't because she was just standing behind him with her arms around her waist, watching him, loving him. Damn. He should just tell her he loved her. Maybe he did. Maybe that what the thing that he was afraid of.

He turned and reached out for her, but she shook her head.

"Don't you lie to me. Even to make me feel better," she warned.

He dropped his hand. "I won't. But I hate hurting you."

"I've been hurt before and no doubt this isn't easy on you."

It wasn't but that didn't really seem to matter much to him. The pain that he felt was all for her. He hated that he'd done this. This was what he was. Sure he was good in the sack and fun to hang out with but when the going got tough, this was all he had to give.

Heartbreak and pain.

"I'll sleep in my truck tonight and arrange for my camper to be brought back—"

"No. Not until my parents leave. I don't want to have to answer any questions and we still have your brother's wedding."

Shocked that she'd still go with him he almost asked her if she was sure but the look in her eyes kept him silent.

"Would it be better if I just left?" he asked.

"No—" Her voice broke and she took a couple of deep breaths. "No."

She turned and walked into the camper and he stayed where he was. Just watching her shadow moving and hearing her voice as she talked to Shep. He heard the shower turn on and waited there, confused as to what he should do next.

He'd hurt her more deeply than he imagined and the pain in her voice when she'd told him to stay while her parents were here... He'd never imagined he would make her feel ashamed of them. But he had.

He felt like he was drowning and had forgotten how to swim. All the skill he'd cultivated in his life had provided him with endless entertainment and he thought that made him a well-rounded man, but he was starting to see that it hadn't. He'd just filled his soul with knowledge and stuff but when he needed to be a man of substance, he was still empty.

Tonight he felt that emptiness more than he had in a long time. He rubbed the top of his head and watched the camper and realized that somehow Colby had been filling it and he hadn't acknowledged it.

But he knew that she wasn't going to be there forever and nor should she be. She deserved a man who loved her. A man who could tell her he loved her and build a future with her.

COLBY SHOWERED AND climbed into her bed alone. Waiting for Ollie to come into the camper. She hadn't realized how devastating this was going to be. When Billy left, she'd thought she'd been heartbroken, but she knew now she hadn't been. That had been an infatuation—absolutely nothing like what she felt for Ollie.

Where was he?

She didn't want to look out of the window and see if he was still by the fire. She'd left the window open in the bathroom, so she knew his truck hadn't left. He was still here. And that was both a relief and the absolute worst.

She had always been touted for her strength and of course she was happy she was strong and resilient but at this moment she hated it. She didn't want to be strong. She wanted to curl into a ball and cry until her broken heart didn't hurt anymore. But she couldn't.

She heard the door on the camper open and she let out a sigh of relief. She'd honestly been afraid that he was going to leave, and she'd have to somehow explain to her parents where he'd gone. And to the rodeo people who had all noticed when they'd started living together.

She pulled her pillow closer and buried her face in it as she started crying. She didn't cry silently or quietly, never had. Instead, the harder she tried to quiet it, the louder it seemed.

She heard his footsteps coming toward the bedroom at the end of the camper and held her breath. She wasn't sure she was ready to see him. He stopped and she had to let her breath out and it was loud and jagged.

"I need to get my clothes," he said.

Just those simple and practical words. Of course he did. Why hadn't she thought to put clothes out when she'd set up the bed on the fold-down table? Because she wasn't thinking right now. She was reacting and moving through this as if she were underwater.

"Of course," she said. She sat up and pulled her knees to her chest as the door opened. He didn't turn on the light, which was a small blessing.

He went quickly to the drawers he'd been using and opened them, taking out clothes, and she just watched. Remembering the number of times when he'd done it in the past, and they'd been talking and laughing about their day.

He glanced over at her, his eyes troubled, his profile so strong that it was hard for her to look at him. She closed her eyes, not wanting to see him. But in her mind's eye there he was. That strong jaw, the mouth that she'd kissed so many times, the face that she'd loved long before she'd truly knew him.

She opened her eyes, and he was still there, just waiting.

"I'm sorry."

Of course, he was. He wasn't a monster. He was just a man. A man who didn't love her and had done his best to try to. Right?

"Okay."

Normally she always said it was fine when someone apologized but this wasn't fine. This was never going to be fine. Sure, she'd known what she was getting into when she'd agreed to do him this favor, but she'd always believed...that she'd get what she wanted.

She had never been the type of woman to give up or to back down. So...hadn't anticipated this ending.

"It's not okay, is it? I don't know how to make this right," he said as he sat on the end of the bed. He reached out to touch her and she drew herself back.

His hand dropped and he shook his head. "So we're like

that?"

"I just can't tonight. Tomorrow it'll be better. Different. You'll see. I'll be more myself. Tonight, I'm just a big broken girl. And I need some time," she said. She was crying again, and her voice sounded like it belonged to an ogre that had been hiding under a bridge for decades. Low, scratchy and the words barely discernable.

"Hell, Colby, I never meant for this to happen," he said. "I hate to see you this way."

She pressed her face into her knees because she couldn't stop crying and that wasn't the woman she believed herself to be. "I hate it too."

He didn't say anything else, but she heard him moving, getting off the bed and then a few minutes later she heard the shower come on and lifted her head. Rubbed the heels of her hands over eyes and tipped her head back.

He didn't love her. That was it. She'd known it when he'd asked her for a favor and had allowed herself to believe something that had never been true. She'd fallen for the charade that they'd been playing for his family and friends. She'd even duped her family into believing that there was more between them than friendship.

But there hadn't been.

She'd been the one to make it more. He'd never lied to her so she really didn't have a reason to be mad at him.

Except he'd made love to her like he was never going to let her go. He'd made her feel like they belonged to each other. And now she realized that she'd been the only one to feel like they belonged with each other.

He'd just been doing what he had asked her to do. Doing what he had to in order to make the illusion of their fake engagement seem more real to everyone around them. In the past she might have thought she wasn't loveable or that the flaw was somehow inside of her, but now she was forced to admit she might just have really bad judgment when it came to men.

Certainly, Olivier Rossi wasn't who she'd thought him to be. The man she'd always thought she loved wasn't afraid of emotion or commitment. She'd never seen that in him until tonight.

HE WISHED THERE was a way to turn down the voices in his head. The ones that told him he'd screwed up. That all he had to do was go back to Colby and take her in his arms. Somehow that would make it all okay, except it wouldn't.

He knew he had to find some answers inside of himself. Put to rest whatever the emptiness was that kept driving him to ruin every chance at happiness he had.

The boy he'd been in college hadn't wanted the life that Mia had laid out in front of them, but with Colby it was different. He did want a life with her. Didn't he?

His shower wasn't really helping to clear his head and he didn't want to go back into the camper. He'd seen the tears in her eyes, heard them in her voice when she'd spoken to him. That had cut him to the core.

This is what his emptiness had wrought and he knew better than to pretend there was anything else at play here. He'd done this.

He hadn't meant for her to fall in love with him. He could give himself a pass on that, but then couldn't because he liked the fact that she loved him. He knew he couldn't stay with the rodeo but just leaving wouldn't do either. He had to make sure there was a clown who could cover for him. He wouldn't leave Colby while her parents were here either.

He would be a man about this. Make things as right as he could and then do his soul-searching. Because he knew that whatever the broken thing was inside of him, it must be more deeply damaged than he'd ever supposed. Why else would he walk away from her?

The camper was quiet and dark when he came back out of the shower and he stood there, glancing back at the bed he'd shared with her. She was lying on her side. He couldn't tell if she was sleeping or not, but she didn't say anything so he knew she didn't want to talk to him.

He finished toweling off his hair and walked to the bed she'd made for him. Shep was already sleeping on the end of it and he climbed up next to the dog. Her dog. Everything that mattered to him was hers or tied to her. This old dog that was ornery and sweet, the rodeo…

Was he missing something?

Surely love would feel like a bolt of lightning. Wouldn't it?

He heard her moving around on the bed and remembered the night before when he'd been next to her. Had pulled her into his arms and under him and made love to her until they both fell into a satiated sleep.

His body hardened but he ignored it. She wasn't his. Not now.

He couldn't stay here. He knew she wanted him to stick around but he couldn't sleep inside the camper this close to her. He got up and pulled on his jeans and T-shirt and then put on his boots without socks because he hadn't thought to get them from the dresser earlier and went outside.

As soon as the door closed behind him, his chest felt too tight and it was hard to breathe. Was he having a panic attack?

He walked away from their camp toward the field that was empty and even though it was dark, the light of the moon provided some guidance. As he walked away from her his thoughts coalesced. He knew what he had to do.

He pulled out his phone and called a friend who was a rodeo cowboy and asked him if he could take Ollie's next few shows. After some sleepy conversation, his friend agreed. That was one easy fix. He walked back to his truck and dug one of his sketchbooks out of the glove box and drew Colby.

Colby riding around the barrels as smoothly and seamlessly as she navigated life. He took his time with the sketch, making each line perfect, and when he was done and her image was looking up at him, he knew he couldn't stay.

He knew he'd said he would but there was no way he could fake that nothing had changed between them and he had the feeling that it was only going to make it more apparent to her family and their friends that something had changed.

He knew he was taking the coward's way out but he had made up his mind. He flipped the sketch over and left a note for her. At first he wasn't sure how to start it or what to say but then words flowed.

> *Colby-girl,*
>
> *I'm sorry for doing this after I said I wouldn't. But I need to get away and sort things out in my head and in my heart. No one has ever affected me the way you have these last few months. I know you will use your strength to get through this and it hurts me that I've put you in that position.*
>
> *Ollie*

He wasn't sure she'd forgive him for leaving but he couldn't stay. That was it. He slipped the note into the camper and then got in his truck and left. He had no destination in mind, no place that he really called home except the rodeo and that was gone now. He wouldn't go back to the one place where she was. The one place that was her sanctuary.

He just drove until the sun came up and waited to see if she'd call, but she didn't. Colby wasn't the kind of woman to cry after a man. That she'd cried for him at all was stark and made him realize that he might have lost the one chance he had to make this right. But he was determined to fix himself and find his way back to her.

Chapter Seventeen

"I CAN'T BELIEVE he just left like that," Beckett said as she opened one of the kitchen boxes that Colby's dad had brought in a few hours ago.

Looking around the kitchen in Jasmine Cottage, Colby tried not to dwell too deeply on that fact either. She hadn't expected it but from what he'd told her maybe she should have.

She'd ridden but her heart wasn't in it and facing her rodeo friends she'd felt the absence of Ollie even more, so she'd canceled the rest of the season and come home to Georgetown and bought Jasmine Cottage. It had been too many weeks. Nico and Cressida's wedding was the last weekend in June...next weekend.

Angelica had been calling and had driven over last weekend for dinner to try to convince Colby to come to the wedding. Ollie's family were very sweet people, but they were his family, and she truly wanted no part in their lives without him.

"I can believe it," she said. It made it easier to just stop questioning every move he'd made. If she just took him at face value and forgot the man she'd spent so many hours in conversation with or made love to until she felt their souls touched, then maybe she'd be able to move forward.

"Liar," Beckett said, not unkindly, as she stopped unwrapping the antique glass water goblets that Colby had inherited from her grandmother.

"You're right. But if I think about it too much, I start crying and that's not me. I wish I could just be mad at him. You know that would be a thousand times easier. But I'm not," she said, shaking her head. She was staring at a box of rodeo cups that her mom had saved from when she was a girl.

"I get it. Men suck," she said with a wink going to pour them both a glass of iced tea.

"Men don't suck. Love sucks. There should be some sort of cosmic protection that keeps one person from falling for someone who can't fall in love with you."

But did she really want that? As much as she was miserable now, for a few weeks in spring and early summer she'd been really happy. That was the hard part. The Ollie she'd thought she knew wasn't faking that happiness. So how could he leave her the way he had?

She had to agree that the house coming on the market after all those family visits had to feel like too much pressure to him, but at the same time…it had felt like a sign to Colby. Like they had both found the person who they were meant to be with.

She took the iced tea from Beckett. Her sister one-arm hugged her and Colby took a second to rest her head on her sister's shoulder. She felt sad and wistful at the thought that this place could have been the start of something with Ollie. But the truth was if he didn't want to be here she didn't want him.

"So what are you going to do now? Are you done with the rodeo?" Beckett asked.

"I am for now. I might do the rodeo in Last Stand because that's fun and close. I have a few feelers out. I applied to work in the professional rodeo department at Kelly Boots. Not sure I want to work for a company. Angelica offered me a job at her boutique, which was sweet, but I don't want to do retail."

She had enough money in savings to just let things ride for six months but she knew once she finished her renovation projects at the cottage she'd be bored. "I had an email from Reba Blue. She wants to start a barrel racing school and she has tons of property. I kind of like the idea of that. I'm going to talk to her next week."

"That sounds like something right up your alley. She lives over in Whiskey River too?"

"Yeah. She married a bull rider and that's where his kin are. They have a little girl. She's cute as can be." Colby realized she was rambling but that was all she had. Reba and Nick had something that Colby knew she'd wanted for herself, but she wasn't going to dwell on it.

She'd promised herself she was getting over Ollie Rossi and here she was months later. No closer to falling out of love with him and feeling broken and lost. She was determined to move on.

"Cool," Beckett said. Sounding like she had something else on her mind. "Um, so have you heard from him?"

She thought of the text he'd sent. Just one a week after he'd left. It was longer than the letter he'd left. But still not long enough.

Again, I'm so sorry for leaving. I just have to find some answers.

That hadn't really helped at all. She'd thrown her phone across the room, scaring Shep and cracking the screen. Which wasn't great.

"Nope," she said. "But really what good would it be if he did contact me?"

Beckett put her hands on her hips. "I'm just thinking that maybe the dumbass would have an awakening and realize he'd thrown away the second-best woman in the world."

She smiled at her sister's fierce devotion of her and her ego. "That would be nice. But so far nothing. I think I have to let him go. I mean I know I do. It's just that falling out of love is hard, Becks. I keep trying to tell myself he's not coming back but in the middle of the night I'm reaching for him."

She felt those tears at the backs of her eyes and knew she

had to stop. But her sister was the one person she could say this to. And it felt good to let it out. "I know that makes me sound like a loser—"

"Don't say that. You're not one. You're a woman who loves hard and deep. He's going to realize it sooner or later and that will be his heartache. Don't beat yourself up for loving him."

She smiled, feeling a little bit better. Her sister was right. Love wasn't wasted. She had those good memories and over time she knew this heartache would lessen and she'd be able to think of him without tears.

Or so she hoped.

SIX WEEKS WAS a long time to be away from Colby, Ollie realized. He'd started out trying to find an easy or simple answer to why he'd panicked when she'd mentioned buying a house but there wasn't one. Not a simple one.

Whatever it was that was empty in him felt emptier as he'd driven further from her. But he was a bit hardheaded so it had taken him some time to realize what the answer was.

He'd turned to her a dozen times in the cab of his truck to point out something he thought she'd like, only to be faced with that empty seat. He was listening to The Weeknd way more than he liked but the artist's music reminded him of Colby and the first night they'd slept together.

He'd stopped back by the rodeo last week and been

shocked to learn that Colby had left after he had and many of the regulars told him in no uncertain terms that they blamed him. He took the blame, knowing it was his fault.

He missed his cowgirl and he wanted to get back to her. He'd finally figured out that he'd never been roaming over the country because there was something broken or damaged inside of him. Part of it he'd acknowledged was habit but the other part, which he'd slowly figured out was Colby. She'd been the reason why he'd stayed with the rodeo for so many seasons, she'd been the one person he couldn't wait to get back to and she was the woman he wanted by his side.

He had done some deep soul-searching, something he normally didn't like to do but it had needed to be done. Nico had tracked him down to make sure he was okay. The entire family was worried about him. So he'd driven to Manhattan where Nico was wrapping up business for the summer and the two of them were now driving back to Texas together.

"What are you going to say to her?" Nico asked.

"I don't know. She might not even see me," Ollie reminded his brother.

"I'd lead with I'm an ass and you deserve better," Nico advised.

"Is that how you got Cressida to fall for you?" Ollie asked. His brother was the calmest that Ollie had ever seen him and couldn't wait to get back to Texas and the woman who'd be his wife in a few short days. Seeing Nico and Jock so settled and happy had played into Ollie's thinking while he'd been trying to figure out if he could commit himself to Colby and a future together.

"No. I didn't fuck up the way you did," Nico said dryly.

"You did it a different way?"

Nico laughed and nodded. "Yes. Falling for a woman just messes with your head and it takes a big man to finally let down his guard and admit it."

"I'm trying," he said.

"So what are you going to say to her?" Nico asked again after more miles had passed. "And why are we listening to The Weeknd? I'm putting on ZZ Top."

"No, don't. It reminds me of Colby."

Nico nodded and stopped searching through the playlist on his phone. "Have you let her know you are coming back?"

"No."

"Why not?" Nico asked. "I think that would help your case."

Maybe. But this was Colby. She might still be pissed at him, which was totally justified. "What if she doesn't want to see me? If I show up, she'll at least have to talk and maybe listen to me."

"Dude, you are a mess. But I get it. Falling in love with Cressida was the scariest thing I've ever done. Telling her was the second. There was that moment when I didn't know if she'd say it back or if she felt it...They were the longest seconds of my life, waiting for her to respond."

Waiting for a response…he had just let Colby tell him she loved him and then left it there between them. "Uh, would you have forgiven Cressida if she'd said she needed time?"

"Did you do that? Please tell me you're smarter than that."

"I'm not. Yes, I did that. But it was only because I wanted to be sure," he said. But even as he was trying to justify it to his brother, it sounded lame. Colby had said she loved him, had asked him to meet her halfway and he'd been unable to. He'd been too stymied by fear to give her the one thing she needed from him.

"You're f—ed."

"I know. And it's taken me six weeks to come back… She's probably moved on."

"She probably hasn't. If she is truly in love with you, she hasn't. And I would have forgiven Cressida. In fact I would have just bided my time and come back again and again until she realized she was in love with me too. I knew that she was the one for me. And if it had taken the rest of my life to convince her of that, then so be it."

Hearing his brother speak so plainly about the woman he loved reassured Ollie that there was still a chance he could fix things with Colby. It might take him the next ten months or even the next ten years but he wasn't going to give up. He'd finally realized what had been missing in his life and he refused to give her up now.

When they got to Whiskey River, Ollie dropped Nico off at Cressida's house and then had to decide where to go. It took about thirty seconds for him to point his truck toward Georgetown and the one woman he needed.

BECKETT HAD GONE home. Colby was spending the first night in her new home. Despite the heat she was sitting out on the wide porch that ran the length of the front of the house in the large wooden swing that her dad had helped her hang. In one of her old boxes had been the portable CD player her grandparents had given her when she was in middle school and a mix CD she'd made when she'd been a senior in high school.

She'd felt a pang as she'd seen her handwriting on the CD. *Colby's Feel Good Mix*. That girl had no idea what life had in store for her. And listening to the music now, Colby decided that just like Jo Dee Messina she was doing all right. It had been a near thing a couple of times. When Billy had left and made her feel the fool. That was a mistake she wished she'd never made.

If she hadn't then maybe she would have been more open when she'd met Ollie. But she was still hurt and by the time she'd realized that he was different...but was he? She was forced to face the fact that she was rewriting their story already. Maybe this was how she was going to get over him.

But that wasn't happening today, she thought as she took another sip of the Lynchburg lemonade she'd mixed up after dinner. It felt like a drinking night to her. She wanted to establish the habit of sleeping through the night without Ollie at Jasmine Cottage.

And drinking...well that was one way to ensure she fell asleep quickly. But staying asleep, she knew was going to be harder. The neighborhood was quiet. Earlier some kids had been riding their bikes but now everyone was either inside or doing something else.

Except her.

She told herself that she didn't need to be busy, that this was the way to heal. Stopping and thinking. Acknowledging the emotions she still felt no matter how much she wished she didn't.

Shep was sleeping by her feet as a familiar truck pulled into her drive. Shep perked up but she put her hand on his collar, keeping him by her side. "Stay."

He did but she could feel that he wanted to run to Ollie and say hi to the friend he'd missed. Hell, she didn't blame him—she wanted to run to him too. It was only self-preservation, stubbornness and a little bit of fear that kept her seated.

He turned off the truck and sat there, hands resting on the steering wheel, aviator-frame sunglasses covering his eyes as he looked over at her. She just raised her glass to him and took a long swallow of her drink. Then immediately regretted it. Drunk, she might say something she'd regret.

She might tell him how good he looked. And as he got out of the cab of his truck and walked toward her, she realized he looked damned good. His faded, old jeans, clung to his thighs, his T-shirt—an old rodeo one—did the same to his muscled chest. He wasn't wearing a cowboy hat so she could see his hair was shaggy and longer. He could use a haircut, but it didn't detract from his looks.

He stopped at the base of the two steps that led up to her porch. Shep started whining and it was only his training that kept him by her side. She finally relented and waved her hand in a signal he knew meant he could leave his position at her side.

She watched her dog go and shower his love on the one other person he truly loved. Told herself she wasn't going to do the same thing. In fact she realized as she saw him standing there as if nothing had happened that there was a good chance she might punch him.

She hadn't realized how strong the impulse was until her nails dug into her palms and she relaxed her hand.

"At least someone is happy to see me," Ollie said, still not moving from the bottom step.

"He is happy to see the mailman so I wouldn't let it go to your head," she responded. She hated that she got like this when she was mad at him. She felt that meanness deep inside and her rational mind knew that this wasn't going to make her feel better, but she couldn't help it.

"Fair enough," he said. "Uh, can I come up and talk to you?"

"It's a free country."

"Colby."

Just her name but she heard the rebuke in his tone.

"Ollie," she said back, but in her voice, she heard the loneliness and the longing that she hadn't been able to shake even though he'd left her.

"You left me. You said you wouldn't, but you did it anyway," she said. Once she started talking, she felt that stir of tears, but she controlled them. She refused to cry in front of him again. "Why?"

He rubbed his hand over the top of his hair and then put his hands in his back pockets. "I'm an idiot and more of an ass than I'd realized."

She knew he was inviting her to let her guard down and let him in again, but she wasn't going to be easily led this time. She had loved him for so long and his leaving should have broken his hold on her but sitting here waiting to throw herself at him the way Shep had told her it hadn't.

"And?"

"Can we talk? Really talk. Not you answering me in one-word comments," he asked.

She took a deep breath. This might be it. Her last chance to do this with him and get the closure that they both needed. And who was she kidding? She wanted to talk to him. To have him get closer to her so she could smell his aftershave and maybe touch him.

She'd missed him even though she hadn't wanted to.

Chapter Eighteen

S HE LOOKED GOOD, strong. His cowgirl wasn't fading away, but he could tell from the way she'd spoke to him that her outer image didn't match what was going on beneath the surface. She was sort of like a misty Texas morning to him. He couldn't see everything that was out there but he knew he'd love it all.

He loved her. If he'd figured out one thing on the road it was that. But now that he was here, he was acting like he'd never faced thousands of pounds of raging bull...honestly he'd rather. He started sweating and his skin felt too tight. He felt like he was fourteen again and everything about himself was weird or odd.

"Sure we can talk. I'll stop giving you a bitchy answer to everything you say. Want some Lynchburg lemonade?"

That answer just made him love her even more. "You have every right to be bitchy. We just can't move forward if you keep treating me the way I deserve to be."

Her eyes narrowed and she tipped her head to the side as she studied him. He felt like she was sizing him up and for the first time he realized he was standing before her completely vulnerable. She might not recognize it but he was. He'd let his guard down around her a long time ago but hadn't realized it until he'd left her.

"That's true. Lemonade?"

"Sure," he said.

"It's in the fridge and there are glasses on the counter. And I could use a refill," she said, handing him her glass.

He took it. Their fingers brushed and a sizzle went through him. Screw it.

He put the glass on the table next to her swing and took her hand in his. He wasn't going to waste any more time. He didn't want a drink or anything else unless it came with Colby.

She seemed startled by his move and tried to pull her hand back but he kept it, rubbing his thumb over the backs of her knuckles and going down on one knee. She raised both eyebrows at that and shook her head.

"Get up."

"No, I can't," he said. Realizing there was a very real possibility that she might cast him aside. Tell him he was too late. And that didn't matter any more than a charging bull did when he jumped in the ring with his clown makeup on and distracted it from a fallen bull rider.

He wished he had that makeup on now, but that would just be one more way he was hiding from her and he wasn't doing that anymore.

"Colby-girl, I know that words aren't good enough to

apologize for what I did. I broke my word to you, something I swore I wouldn't do. And the reasons seemed strong to me at the time, but I know that's not going to hold water."

She stopped trying to pull her hand away and leaned closer to him so that their faces were only a few inches apart. "You did what you had to do. I don't understand it, but if I know anything about you it's that you don't break your word easily."

That was a relief. He didn't want her to think that everything about him was a lie. "Thank you for that. It's more than I deserve."

"It's not. Listen, if we are going to move forward, let's stop apologizing about who we are. I shouldn't have just dropped the L word on you the way I did, you shouldn't have left after I did it but both us were pushed to a spot where that was the only path. What I really need to know is why are you here now?"

He stood up and sat down next to her on the swinging bench, turning so they were facing each other. "I…"

God, now that it was time to say the words out loud they were caught in the back of his throat and he hesitated.

She frowned. "Are you here because you want me to go to your brother's wedding with you?"

He frowned back at her. "No. I'm here because… Let me start over. I left because I always felt like there was something missing inside of me. Growing up I was the odd son, the one who was just a bit different. In college I started to find my footing and then when Mia and I got engaged, I didn't fit in with her version of a groom or future husband. Then I came to the rodeo and met you. And you, rightly so, suggested we just be friends. And we were...are?"

She sighed and chewed her lip. "I don't know yet."

"Fair enough," he said. "When I left it was because I thought that emptiness inside of me was still there and that I had nothing to fill it with. That I was broken in some way that made it impossible for me to truly love you," he said.

Then he paused to think through his words. If ever there was a time when he needed to be confident it was now. She needed to know how he felt and that he had no doubts.

"It didn't take me long to realize that was a mistake," he said. "That the emptiness wasn't a lack of ability to love, but a fear of letting myself. I love you, Colby Tucker. I came back now because I was hoping you'd find it in your heart to forgive me. And maybe you still might love me too."

That was it. The words seemed to linger in the air around them. It felt like a million years were passing but she said nothing. She licked her lips and tipped her head to the side, her eyes narrowing.

"So now you love me?"

"I do. I'm prepared for you to have doubts but know this—I'm giving you my word that you're the only woman I want in my life, the only woman I've ever truly loved and if you believe tonight or a year from now, that won't change."

∽

COLBY WAS ALMOST afraid to believe what she heard. Almost. She had been waiting to hear these words from him for too long. She didn't want to pretend she wasn't still in love with him. But her trust in him had been bruised and she hated it but she needed some reassurance.

The sun was setting and the automatic lights on the street were coming on and she knew it wouldn't be long until the mosquitos were out, but she reached over and flipped on the mosquito candle in a warmer near the swinging bench, but she knew it was a distraction. She wasn't sure what to say to him.

She wanted to just say hell yeah and throw herself in his arms, but she also didn't want to be alone and scared and broken again in a year because she hadn't been realistic with herself.

It was hot, but the heat didn't bother her, as it gave her something else to think about other than the fact that her entire future with Ollie hinged on the next few minutes.

Minutes were going to decide what happened next between them.

"What changed your mind?" she asked. She was trying to be cautious, to be smart but this was a matter of heart, and no rationale was needed. She wanted to believe. Just needed a little more information before she did.

"It was the fried apples at Cracker Barrel and the smell of jasmine when I stopped at a rest area to stretch my legs. The sunset that was so beautiful all filled with pinks and purples.

I kept turning to share it with you and you weren't there."

These were all things that she loved; she hadn't realized he'd noticed them but maybe she would have if they hadn't been pretending with each other so much of the time. It was hard not to believe him when he was saying all the right things and this was Ollie so she knew in her gut he wouldn't lie like that.

"Then one day I thought: I'm out here on the road searching for answers and all I'm finding is the ghost of you...I hadn't known what I'd find but I found you."

Her heart was in her throat as he just kept talking and explaining but she didn't need to hear anything else. He had found her.

"I found you too," she admitted. "I immediately put you in the friend zone because I didn't trust myself and wasn't ready to be hurt again by another smooth-talking cowboy, but I fell for you anyway. I do love you, Ollie."

"I love you too. I wish I'd realized it when you told me the first time. Can you ever forgive me?" he asked, turning to look at her, and she noticed the sincerity in his eyes and those laugh lines. She reached up to touch his face.

"I already have," she admitted.

He stood up and lifted her into his arms and walked to the house.

"What are you doing?"

"First I'm going to make love to you, then I'm going to hold you and talk about our future, then make love to you again," he said. "That work for you?"

"Yes," she said, wrapping her arms around his neck and kissing him. The kiss was the first one they'd shared since they both admitted their love and it hit her deep in her soul. This man was hers. She knew it wouldn't just be smooth sailing for them but that was the fun of the ride.

He carried her inside and Shep followed closely on their heels, going to settle down on his bed in the kitchen. Ollie set her on her feet.

"I want to see your dream house," he said, but he couldn't keep his hands off of her.

"Let's start in the bedroom," she said, leading him down the short hallway to her bedroom. She had an antique wrought-iron headboard that fit the queen-sized bed. The quilt on it had been made by her mama when she'd graduated college and the pillows...well they were from her camper and one of them smelled like Ollie.

He took her in his arms, kissing her as he lowered her back on the bed. He made love to her thoroughly, taking his time to kiss every inch of her skin and when she pushed his shirt off his shoulders, she noticed that his tattoo had been modified. She pushed him to his side so she could get a closer look.

It now read: *Colby owns this Tin Man's heart.*

"You own mine too," she admitted. "When did you have this done?"

"About a week after I left you. I was in Santa Monica and staring at the ocean, realizing that I could be staring at nothing without you by my side."

"A week. What'd you do for the rest of the time?" she asked.

"Tried to figure out how to prove to you that I was sincere. That this time I meant what I said. I knew we both needed time to be sure. So I just kept searching and each time the only thing I found were things you loved. Things I wanted to share with you."

"Oh, Ollie."

"I love you, Colby-girl, your love is the best gift I've ever received," he said.

They spent the rest of the night as he'd said. Making love and talking about the future and it turned out that Ollie might have thought he hadn't planned for the future, but he had a lot of ideas for the two of them.

Which suited her just fine.

They called their families the next day and everyone was happy for them. But Colby knew that the real happiness came when they were alone in each other's arms. It was what she'd wanted for so long and now she finally had it.

The End

Want more? Don't miss Angelica and Max's story in *Christmas with the Texas Billionaire*!

Join Tule Publishing's newsletter for more great reads and weekly deals!

Acknowledgements

Special thanks to Sinclair Sawhney for her deft editing skills and for always being excited when Nick Blue shows up in a book. Also my heartfelt appreciation for my Zombie Belles—Eve, Lenora, Janet, Denise and Nancy—who always listen to my story worries and cheer me on when I finally finish the story.

If you enjoyed *Smooth Talking Texan*,
you'll love the next book in…

The Rossis of Whiskey River series

Book 1: *Texas Christmas Dare*

Book 2: *Smooth Talking Texan*

Book 3: *Christmas with the Texas Billionaire*
Coming in November 2022

Available now at your favorite online retailer!

More books by Katherine Garbera

The Corbyn Sisters of Last Stand series

Book 1: *Red Hot Texan*
Book 2: *Texas Christmas Baby*
Book 3: *Texan for the Taking*

The Dangerous Delaneys series

Book 1: *Her Texas Ex*
Book 2: *Full Texas Throttle*
Book 3: *Texas Christmas Tycoon*

The Scott Brothers of Montana series

Book 1: *A Cowboy for Christmas*
Book 2: *The Cowboy's Reluctant Bride*
Book 3: *Her Summer Cowboy*
Book 4: *Cowboy, It's Cold Outside*
Book 5: *Her Christmas Cowboy*

Available now at your favorite online retailer!

About the Author

Katherine Garbera is the USA Today bestseller author of more than 115 books. She is celebrating her 25th year as a published author in 2022 and is still thrilled to bring stories of happily ever after to her readers. Her books are known for their emotional impact and sizzling sensuality. She lives in the midlands of the UK (aka not London) with her husband and sweet miniature dachshund.

Thank you for reading

Smooth Talking Texan

If you enjoyed this book, you can find more from all our great authors at TulePublishing.com, or from your favorite online retailer.

TULE
PUBLISHING

CPSIA information can be obtained
at www.ICGtesting.com
Printed in the USA
LVHW042250260422
717240LV00005B/345